DEATH OF THE SNAKE CATCHER

SHORT STORIES

DEATH OF THE SNAKE CATCHER

SHORT STORIES

by Ak Welsapar

Translated by
Lois Kapila, Youssef Azemoun and Richard Govett

Edited by Richard Govett

Cover and interior layout by Max Mendor

© 2018, Ak Welsapar

© 2018, Glagoslav Publications

www.glagoslav.com

ISBN: 978-1-911414-81-0

A catalogue record for this book is available from the British Library.

DEATH OF THE SNAKE CATCHER

AK WELSAPAR

SHORT STORIES

TRANSLATED BY
LOIS KAPILA, YOUSSEF AZEMOUN AND RICHARD GOVETT

GLAGOSLAV PUBLICATIONS

CONTENTS

STORIES FROM A DIVIDED LIFE

Foreword by Ann Morgan

Unless you're a publisher, it's not often that you have the privilege of being one of the first people to read a book. But that was what happened to me in 2012 when I began an email correspondence with Ak Welsapar.

At the time, I was in the middle of a project to try to read a book from every country in the world. It was proving to be an extraordinary, mind-expanding adventure that frequently saw me agonising between many tempting titles in an effort to select just one for each nation.

Not so when it came to Turkmenistan, however. Every time I tried to source an English translation of a literary work from that particular Central Asian state, I found myself hitting a brick wall. There seemed to be nothing available.

Indeed, information on Turkmenistan itself was very hard to come by. Beyond a few cursory articles outlining the physical location of the state – between Kazakhstan, Uzbekistan, Afghanistan, Iran and the Caspian Sea – and the role its ancient metropolis, Merv, played as a staging post on the Silk Road before the nation was absorbed into the Russian Empire and then the Soviet Union, finally achieving independence in 1991, there was very little to go on. The few media reports I found focussed on eccentric decisions by its rulers, such as former life president Saparmurat Niyazov's project to found a penguin sanctuary in the Karakum Desert, and the fact that the capital, Ashgabat, holds the record for the highest density of white marble-clad buildings in the world. Nothing I saw could give me a glimpse of what life might be like for an ordinary Turkmen citizen and there was certainly no mention of literary works by people living there that I might be able to read.

In months of searching, the only promising lead I uncovered was that exiled writer and author of more than 20 books Ak Welsapar was slated to be the Turkmen representative at London's Poetry Parnassus, a gathering of poets from around the globe organised to coincide with the 2012 Olympic

Games. I contacted Welsapar to explain what I was looking for and he generously sent me the manuscript of WM Coulson's translation of the novel that Glagoslav Publications went on to release in 2016 as *The Tale of Aypi*. It was, to his knowledge, the first literary work ever to be translated directly from Turkmen into English.

There's a good reason that we in the anglophone world hear little from Turkmenistan. Ranked 178 out of 180 in Reporters Without Borders' 2017 World Press Freedom Index and with a similarly abysmal human rights record, the autocratic state is one of the most restricted places on the planet. The media is entirely government-controlled and internet access is kept prohibitively expensive for most citizens, with foreign-news and social-media sites banned. In this secretive nation, ruled with the help of a personality cult to rival that of the Kim dynasty in North Korea, criticism of 'The Patron' – simultaneous president, prime minister and commander-in-chief Gurbanguly Berdymukhamedov – is dealt with in the strongest terms. The same was true under Berdymukhamedov's predecessor, Niyazov, as Ak Welsapar knows all too well.

By the time Niyazov assumed power in 1991, when Turkmenistan gained independence from the Soviet Union, Welsapar was well versed in what it meant to live under suspicion. You could almost say it was in his blood. His father had grown up as the son of an enemy of the people, living with the constant threat of exposure and imprisonment, after his own father died in the struggle against the Bolsheviks. This disgrace overshadowed Ak Welsapar's childhood, colouring his interactions with teachers and students, and putting the family under great strain. Visits to relatives in the border village of Miana – home of a historical rebellion against the collective farm system – were forbidden in case they harmed the children's prospects.

But it was in the late 1980s that Welsapar began to feel the full force of what being a dissident writer would mean. A series of articles in which he revealed the chronic malnutrition of the rural population and the devastating impacts of the overuse of chemicals in agriculture led to him being declared an enemy of the people. Then in 1991, youth magazine 'Yashlyk' published his satirical novel 'The Bent Sword on the Old Carpet' and the new Turkmen regime rushed to censor it, excising almost every other paragraph. Unable to tolerate this desecration of his work, Welsapar confronted the chief censor only to discover that, illogically, the department had taken exception to his criticism of the former Soviet system. 'Soviet power was no more, but Turkmen censorship continued to defend the interests of the Communist system and the Red Empire,' he told me when I interviewed him for the book that eventually came out of my international reading project, *Reading the World*.

What followed felt like a return to the darkest days of the Stalin era. Expelled from the writers' union and the union of journalists, Welsapar saw his books removed from libraries and shops, and burned. His blacklisting had a knock-on effect on his personal life: friends and former colleagues began to avoid him in the street. Meanwhile, his wife was fired from her position as a teacher in a primary school and his ten-year-old son was forbidden from continuing his education. After two years, the family had had enough. In 1993, after twelve months under house arrest, the writer fled the country – followed by his family in 1994 – and made his home in Sweden, where Welsapar lives to this day.

The move granted the author the space to write without persecution and, in time, the opportunity to reach an international audience far beyond the scope of what he could ever have achieved in his home country. His work has been published in several languages, including Swedish, Russian and English, and he has received a grant from Human Rights Watch, as well as Ukrainian and Russian literary prizes.

Back in the early 1990s, however, the step seemed potentially devastating. Being separated from his audience – from the people who read his mother tongue – could have spelled the end of Welsapar's career. 'I almost had to start from scratch as a writer during the emigration,' he told me. 'But I had no choice. The choice between emigration and staying in my native country was for me a choice between life and death, and I chose to live.'

Starting from scratch necessitated more than simply thinking of fresh stories to write and learning languages to write them in. 'When a writer starts to write a new work, he or she tries to imagine its potential audience. In my case, the audience I have now is much broader than it was before the emigration. Through losing Turkmenistan, I have found another home – Sweden, and not only that! So now, as I write, I imagine readers from around the world. Because of that, I write so that my works are equally interesting for readers of any country.'

As well as expanding his readership, style and the languages in which he wrote, exile also broadened and deepened Welsapar's grasp of his subject matter. As with so many writers who have resisted attempts to silence them

– from Burkinabé investigative journalist Norbert Zongo to great Russian dissident Aleksandr Solzhenitsyn – his oppressors' actions ended up working against them. Instead of intimidating Welsapar into wordlessness, the repressiveness of the regime that had gripped his homeland merely strengthened his resolve – and gave him plenty more things to write about. In losing his country, Welsapar arguably found, or at least raised, his voice.

The stories featured in this book are testament to the way these experiences have shaped the author's career. Written over many decades – some while Welsapar was still in Turkmenistan and others since he left – and in a variety of circumstances, the pieces are, at first glance, very different. This is not simply a function of them being the work of three different translators: Lois Kapila, Youssef Azemoun and Richard Govett. The mechanisms at work in the stories are themselves very varied. While some display mythic qualities, others are rooted in specific times and places, and make reference to particular political events. The rules differ between the worlds evoked: dogs can talk in one and in another the dead have the power to conjure a sea mist.

Yet, although the stories may appear very diverse, a closer look reveals a number of common themes and tropes at work. The power of the unexplained is among the most prominent. As in *The Tale of Aypi*, a book that is haunted by the ghost of a girl who died some centuries before the story takes place, the uncanny has a strong influence. The ground shifts constantly beneath our feet, leaving us uncertain what to expect and what to trust. In 'On the Emerald Shore', the tale in the collection that most recalls the novel, we are left doubtful as to what is real as the narrator quests around for the explanation of a young man's drowning. Perhaps in this story's universe it is possible for people to predict their own deaths, as some of those discussing the incident suggest. Maybe the dead really can control the weather. We can never be sure.

In other stories, this sense of uncertainty spreads to engulf everyday objects. People cannot be trusted and neither can things. Even the most innocuous-seeming of occurrences – a love affair, two carts approaching a crossroad, a man writing at a desk – can turn treacherous and become the thing that destroys your life. As Jummi, the luckless team leader in 'One of the Seven is a Scoundrel', says, 'these days one of your two eyes can become your enemy.'

For readers, these sudden shifts in significance are as instructive as they are unsettling. Faced with a reality that may never be quite what it seems, we find ourselves ill at ease. Like a citizen in a society overseen by a fickle dictator, or a writer working in the shadow of freedom of expression-limiting rules the specifics of which are left at the discretion of individual censors – as was the case in the Soviet era – we can never be sure what is safe. It is as though Welsapar writes us into the world he has left, letting us taste the bitterness of living in constant fear of recrimination for offences, or faults in interpretation, we may not even realise we have committed.

In some of the stories, this process is explicit. 'Love in Lilac', for example, takes us through the horror of a romance curdling into a nightmare when student Arslan discovers he has transgressed by falling in love with a foreigner. The most harrowing scene is disturbing precisely because of the way it makes the banal savage: after being hauled out of a lecture by KGB agents, the student is taken to an office in an enormous grey building and made to sit in the corner of a room in which a colonel is writing at a desk. Nothing further happens. And that is precisely what makes the scene so monstrous. As the hours pass and Arslan sits paralysed by his ignorance of what has brought him there and what may be about to take place – to the point that he eventually urinates where he sits rather than asking to go to the toilet – normal everyday objects and activities mutate into instruments of torture. The office environment, the man writing and even the simple act of sitting on a chair become terrible and unknowable – things liable to drive those exposed to them mad in the right circumstances. When at last he is given leave to go, we see the damage that the experience has caused in the way it has robbed Arslan of his ability to engage with quotidian things:

'The town deafened Arslan with the boom and clamour of its usual, frantic rhythm, as if trying to draw him back to normal life. It blinded the young man with countless billboards, emblazoned with enticing names – look, it's life! Come back, breathe, live!

But it wasn't easy to return to normal life. Arslan felt like it was all far away from him now. He felt detached from everything around him. Everything he saw every day and which had made him so happy was beyond him, behind him, not with him.

And the people hurrying by, and the cars rushing along the evening avenues, looked unreal, like playthings. Or was it he, Arslan, who had become a plaything?'

The unease that underpins many of the stories in *The Death of the Snake Catcher* is augmented by Welsapar's use of voices. At times functioning like a kind of Greek chorus, the 'vacationing gossips and tattle-tongues' that comment upon many of the incidents contest and overrule accounts, complicating and contradicting the idea of a single coherent narrative. The truth, we learn, is hard to unpick and may ultimately elude us, or, as the narrator of 'On the Emerald Shore' puts it, 'the most important thing, the secret thing, maybe, slips away as always, and remains unfathomable'.

Unknowability is evident in the ways the stories are told. Sometimes it declares itself and is even the source of humour. The garrulous narrator of 'The Junkman', for example, is forever drawing our attention to the possibility that his facts are incorrect or that there may be another version of events. 'I cannot vouchsafe that it all happened like that, because it was all long before I was born. And I must say my Great Uncle, while being a great lover of recalling various amazing stories from the past, was not famed for his love of the truth, as far as I can remember.' In this piece, with its cast of eccentric characters and frequent nods at other unnarrated scandals and intrigues, the unreliability of what we are reading is part of the fun. Meanwhile, in 'On the Emerald Shore', the narrator exhorts us to 'Judge for yourself: would a father argue with his grown daughter in such a way over a trifle?' almost as if he is absolving himself of any responsibility for drawing conclusions from the events he relates.

The conversational tone in which many of the stories are recounted adds to the play between the familiar and the strange that makes the book by turns so enjoyable and alarming. Drawing on the Turkmen oral tradition, Welsapar gives many of the narratives a cosy, informal air. Characters swap jokes and insults. They complain about their everyday hardships – the challenge of getting food, the problems of the harvest. The mundane feel of many of the exchanges makes the sinister events, when they happen, all the more unnerving. When it is possible for an NKVD official to swoop in and abduct you as you are riding along in the sweltering summer sun and gossiping with your neighbours, it seems nothing is safe.

The impression that many of the scenarios are a sort of waking nightmare is reflected in the dreamlike settings Welsapar devises for them. Although details add specificity in some cases, the majority of the stories in *The Death of the Snake Catcher* take place in a no man's land – 'on a mountain's foothills' or in unnamed communities that seem to be everywhere and nowhere all at once. There is a whimsical, almost other-worldly quality to the landscape as though all the stories – and not just the events in 'Egyptian Night of Fear' – are the product of the world of dreams.

The fable-like nature of some of the tales adds to this. In 'Love Story', for example, the hero's beloved asks him to prove his regard for her by bringing her his mother's still-beating heart, the sort of savage, outlandish quest we might expect to encounter in a fairy tale. Similarly, the final piece in the collection, 'On the Edge', in which the sad fate of the anthropomorphised wolf-hound Alabay represents the tragic lot of the Soviet intelligentsia after the collapse of the USSR, demonstrates the 'Aesopian language' Welsapar told me he grew adept at using to smuggle truths and political points past the censors.

The blurred backdrops and mythic quality that many of the works share reflects the universality that Welsapar strives for in his writing – his desire to produce work that will appeal to readers anywhere in the world. Indeed, in loosening the local ties in his settings, Welsapar gives his stories scope to migrate to the most universal nation of all: the country of exile. Decluttered of all but a few locally specific details – the beloved's role as a sankomissiya charged with checking the cleanliness of her fellow students' hands in 'Altynai', for example, or the old Tula patterns on the lintels in 'Ryazan Horseradish and Tula Gingerbread' – the stories leap free of their context into a nebulous everyland where emotions and human responses take centre stage. There is something of the starkness of the interrogation room in the spare settings Welsapar creates, such that the inhumanity and terrifying inscrutability of the many oppressors who patrol these pages expand to fill the vacuum left by everyday things. Like helpless individuals backed into a corner by the tyrannous regime bent on controlling us, readers can focus on nothing but the immediate threat. We stand with Jummi in 'One of the Seven is a Scoundrel', staring into the NKVD officer's eyes that have become so intense they seem 'to have turned into a whirlpool in a deep sea ready to devour everything'.

Yet, although the stories frequently tackle dark subject matter, there is a lightness to the writing that lifts it out of the gloom that might otherwise swamp these pages. We see it in the optimism of young lovers and in the determination of many of the characters to achieve the dignity of leading an independent existence – no matter how limited and basic that might be. What's more, hopefulness pervades the title story, in which two mortal enemies – the snake catcher and his prey – meet and in so doing discover that they have made each other what they are. Although their identities are built at least partly on their mission to destroy one another, the story hints that the world might nevertheless be big enough to contain them both. As Welsapar explained when I asked him about the collection: 'People should never forget that we are only part of a great life, a cosmos, and it does not become a person to take living space from other living creatures. Only the weak strive to destroy one another. The strong learn to coexist.'

For all the difficulties he and his characters face, the belief that a better reality is possible underpins Welsapar's writing. Just as he continued to work in the face of what must have seemed like insurmountable obstacles when he was first blacklisted and forced to endure seeing his books destroyed, so the people he portrays retain faith that survival is its own reward and that tomorrow may bring better things. Even if 'the most important thing, the secret thing, maybe, slips away as always, and remains unfathomable', the effort to express what can be expressed and live what can be lived is worthwhile.

This optimism in the face of great adversity is the key not only to the stories themselves but to the reason you hold this book in your hands. Through Ak Welsapar's persistence and commitment to his craft, we English speakers now have access to not one but two literary works from Turkmenistan. At last, more than 25 years after the state declared its independence, readers of the world's most published language have a choice of texts that can help us picture how life looks in one of the most hard-to-imagine nations on Earth.

ON THE EMERALD SHORE

Translated by Lois Kapila

"What thing is most reliable?"
"Earth."
"And least?"
"Sea."
Pittacus, a sage of ancient Greece

On the third day, a mist enveloped the sea. Albescent, rising up off the water, it languidly wrapped around the shore, then the town, little by little covering the entire surroundings. People said that it was no coincidence, while Arta, the steward at the holiday house, who for some reason was called "The Hunchback" behind his back, did not mince his words: it was the work of the drowned.

They had already been looking for her for three days, round the clock – but in vain. The search group, hastily thrown together, two amateur divers from the local Sea Wings club, took turns in searching through the water's depths. A policeman and a mechanic, on a grey, ugly, skeletal fishing boat, the Yagmur, moved further and further from the shore. From there, the vacationers watched them, and also carried out their own search. They raked over the waves with their gaze, in the hope that, sooner or later, the drowned girl would wash to shore. Just as he had done...

He had drowned. The sea had swallowed him – an act of vengeance for something. But for what, nobody knew.

Mergen, tall and brown-haired, a sceptic with grey, vapid eyes, immediately said that those who show off, or rather, as he put it, all posers and ponces who come here to holiday and plot evil jokes with the sea, end in this very way. Everybody listened closely to his words, but not everybody agreed. It seemed to me that this was a simplification by Mergen, or maybe he had been offended by the drowned guy, and so now was mocking him.

I continued to think there was something strange in this death, for surely a man such as Charlie, for this was the name of the deceased, could not drown in the shallow waters of the Avaza. His body glistened with health, and spread-eagled on the empty shore, even dead, instilled those around with a quiet respect.

Nevertheless, death came – the medical report later stated, "Cause of death: drowning" – and all of the conversations turned around this. Murad said that it probably wasn't because he swam badly or anything. Sometimes unfortunate things happen, and even the most outstanding swimmers can be swallowed up by the sea. Cramps, for example. Who can claim to be immune to cramps? Maybe the young man had been struck with just that fate?

I observed him closely, as he was talking about the death of this guy he had never met, and realised that he was genuinely grieved. This handsome man, dressed in an imported fabric of the highest quality, always in a bubbly mood, on that evening sat across from me sorrowful and dull. I admit, I suddenly felt ashamed for dismissing this guy as a playboy until now. On top of this, Murad seemed sentimental; admittedly, this seems to be a natural trait in this type. Yet all the same, he astonished me with his extreme sensitivity:

"I can picture the very last moment of his life. He probably said to himself as he died, 'What else can I do to save myself? Nothing. Everything I could do, I have done.'"

And then he unexpectedly turned to me:

"How long does a man live after his death?"

I replied, "Two to three minutes, at most, until the mind cools down. Until that moment, he can hear. That's why, when somebody dies, those who sit around his bed cry with more fervour, so that the dying, or I should say, dead man, believes that those close to him are grieving over him, that they are unhappy."

"So that means," said Murad, "that he battled the waves until his very death and, only having died, his mind turned to those close to him: 'You understand what else I could do? Nothing....'"

And then Murad rushed headlong towards the sea. Adelina did her best to hold him back. I tried to talk him out of it. But he continued to maintain, "What will be will be! Let the sea take me and do with me what it will!"

And with those words, he almost broke down in tears, and became indescribably embarrassed. He missed his wife and his child who were far away at home, without the faintest idea of where he was. But he was not alone here. He said that something terrible could also one day happen to him, and he would ingloriously disappear, cease to exist to those close to him – without trace, without honour...

The sea was agitated throughout the night – it simply did not want to calm. The entire night, we listened to the raging waves beat on the rocky shore.

The following day, we – the regulars at the billiard table at Parus, the only respectable holiday house on the empty Caspian shore – gathered together, and once again talk, of course, turned to the drowned man. Everybody offered different theories. Samed recalled that Charlie had, on that ill-fated day, played billiards for a long time, something that nobody had seen him do before, and he either got into an argument with somebody, or simply being out of sorts, let slip several sad phrases that now seemed very strange and mysterious. According to him, it was as if the deceased could sense some impending disaster and, who knows, maybe even knew about his imminent death?

Samed recounted that it was as if Charlie muttered, "A life without risk is not worth a brass farthing." But somebody disagreed vehemently with him, recalling he had said something different: "Life is only worth anything when you take risks." Whatever he said, everybody agreed about one thing: his demeanour had definitely been somewhat downcast.

Then another young man stepped forward, attempting to bring us from these soaring heights of fancy back to earth. Banal phrases do not have magical powers, or the inexplicable will of fate, he said. Many people, he said, voice that motto and it's a commonplace truth: "Risk is a noble thing," or "He who dares, wins."

But it wasn't that easy for the vacationing gossips and tattle-tongues to put a full stop on this whole affair of the deceased, because too much remained unclear. It was Aman that brought up the topic again – a chubby guy, who, regardless of his ample belly, was something of a sharp-shooter when it came to billiards. He could pot a ball with his eyes closed, doubling it into different pockets, or into one, but in such a way that the other person's ball by the pocket yields to the object ball, and then, if not all the time, certainly sometimes manages also to deflect the cue ball into the opposite pocket. We all marvelled at his skill and when he was lining up to sink a shot, egged him on, good-naturedly chuckling as we watched him get flustered and search for a comfortable position at the edge of the table to rest his giant belly.

Aman only rarely swam, something that was strange for local residents. He always walked along the sandy beach, attracting attention because of his amusingly protruding paunch, which bounced over his unfailingly fashionable trousers – he was a dandy. It seemed like he came to the seaside for the sole purpose of demonstrating his prowess on the billiard table. He now told us that on the very last day, the drowned boy said to him: "All the same, to die on dry land is easier than to perish gulping down salt water, although the sea for some inexplicable reason draws one in."

This recollection stunned all of us because we had by this point come round to the idea that the whole event had been purely an accident. But now ... very true, it all seemed even contrived: twilight, the desolate shore, and most importantly, a storm. So it seems this stranger was preparing himself for death. Maybe he, not without forethought, picked that day, that hour, and that place? Having been one of the first, and as I later found out, of the few to actually see the body of the drowned man, I noticed blood on his right temple. So I couldn't help but have certain thoughts: the craggy shore, boulders, the noise of the waves, the nocturnal emptiness ... who on earth knows what happened?

I tried to dislodge from my memory all details that might relate to the perished man, Charlie, and it seemed as if I inadvertently teased out a link ... the youngest daughter of the Hunchback of Arta was called Jergi. That's what she was called, although that only vaguely resembled a female Turkmen name. Maybe, it is a strange derivation from the name Jamal, or from some other similar name. There she is, Jergi, walking barefoot along the water's edge, you could often see her at the shore, and hear her rapid, Yomut speech. Was she seventeen yet at that point? I doubt it, barely. Rough around the edges but charming because of her youth, she seemed to be a princess on the wild shore where there were so few women. Many stared at her in wonderment. This meant the young creature had an overwhelming sense of pride that was equalled only by the overwhelming anger the looks induced in her spindly father. These glances from mature men directed at his daughter, both flattered and distressed him.

Once, I happened to overhear how coarsely he cursed one holiday-maker because of her. I saw at that moment the rage stored up in that little man with the wart on his nose. His eyes, dark as the night, burned with a violent flame, while with Jergi those same eyes drew you into the unknown distance ... And straight into that panicked situation fell one hapless heart-throb, who risked making a throw-away quip about the young girl's bare calves, unaware that her father was standing right beside her! (Judging by their exchange, the girl, walking past the holiday-maker, unintentionally raised her ankle-length Turkmen dress a little higher than permitted).

Charlie always swam alone, only sometimes an unknown blond woman would appear beside him - not wildly beautiful, but delicate and dainty as Venetian glass. Generally she swam rather badly and would quickly return to the shore. Charlie though was a strong swimmer, and therefore would venture far out from the shore. We often lost sight of him. The idea of competing or chasing after him didn't even come into anyone's head. While he, it seemed, didn't even notice anyone around him.

The emerald shore, the indescribable purity of the water – it is unlikely you'll find this at the Baltic or the Black Sea. Only here, the unbelievable heat wears down holiday-makers so much that after just two weeks they care about very little, and will desperately run wherever they can to find some cool relief.

The billiard room, where, as I have already said, all of the men (and two or three European women) gathered, was the only place where you could wind down, as it was cooled by Japanese air conditioners. Here, people generally took cover from the swelter of the midday heat.

Charlie didn't go to the billiard room that often, seeming to prefer to spend time alone on the shore, gathering rare rocks or, sitting under a parasol, simply gazing contemplatively out to sea. When I later thought about it, it seemed to me that Jergi had also been there doing the same, but she, in my opinion, was more fond of shells, out of which she would try to fashion necklaces to wear. Only once did I notice her give something to Charlie, laughing and staring deep into his eyes. Maybe she was giving him shells?

As for the tragedy, which had played out on the emerald shore, by the fifth day a great deal had already become clearer to me – and even if it had not become clearer, then, in any case, I had now put my finger on one obvious link between the episode and the wrath of the Hunchback of Arta. Judge for yourself: would a father argue with his grown daughter in such a way over a trifle? It came about like this...

One day as the evening was drawing near, I lay on the shore. It was almost time for dinner, and I was summoning my energy to get up, when from the other side of the enormous boulder next to which I had taken shelter, voices suddenly rang out. The pounding of the sea drowned them out, yet every now and then fragments of phrases reached my ear, and indeed it was shameful to eavesdrop on the conversation of others. I don't know what prevented me from getting up immediately and leaving, but I, having pulled my shirt back on already, stayed there for a while.

"Why are you always hanging around the shore?" I heard an irritated male voice say.

"It's none of your business!" answered a girl, defiantly.

I then recognized them – it was the Hunchback and his daughter.

"How is it none of my business?" asked the Hunchback, in a dull tone.

Jergi answered with extreme irritation:

"I said it isn't any of your business, so it isn't any of your business!"

"Who on earth do you…" The crescendoing drumming of the surf prevented me from hearing the end of the sentence.

"Mother…" She said something else too, but the rising sounds of the waves, drowned out her response.

I continued to listen.

"Your mother? Hardly!" a muffled, malign laugh. "I had almost managed to forget her. Won't you jog my memory a little?"

"Maybe you've forgotten…"

"If I have forgotten, then there's no way you can remember. Besides, she was also … like that. She tortured me, regretted … that she had married."

"As if you had any doubt…"

I admit that I couldn't help but find it interesting, this window into the relationship between the Hunchback, who I had known now for several swimming seasons, and his wife, whose death gave rise to all manner of legends. Rumour had it she had killed herself.

At this point, the exchange between father and daughter turned into a blazing argument.

"I'm sorry to say that I now understand her completely. I'm already grown up…"

"Don't get me angry. You know that would be bad idea…" The wind carried scraps of his vile curses in my direction.

"You're just jealous." She said something about harassment, either on the part of her father, or on the part of holiday-makers.

"If only you had a brother," Arta answered her, "he'd have taken care of this. But it falls to me."

"Your good mother," Arta spat every word with spite, with resentment, "did everything to make sure you were the only child she bore. Right up until it killed her – one step too far with her sorcery and ruses. She wanted to kill the child she was carrying under her heart, but killed herself. She'll burn in hell forever."

"Don't you dare say such evil things about my mother!"

It seemed to me that Jergi had begun to cry. Poor thing, I thought about the long-deceased woman.

The Hunchback continued wilfully:

"Nevertheless, you're …"

"He promised to marry me."

She pronounced these words slowly, with some deep-seated ardour and grievance. I admit I found it all disturbing. What on Earth was this conversation about? I, in any case, lay down on the sand, having taken my shirt off again: I wondered if they could see me, but I, unable to catch what they are saying, lay there quietly.

"He isn't the first," snarled the father. "You're bringing shame on my good name. And who among them will answer for the rest?" Arta cleared his throat, and it seems, once again his talk tailed off with a barrage of curses.

"Hey! Don't threaten me!"

"You don't give a damn while my heart is breaking, I feel sickened. I'm surrounded by people just waiting to get me. My daughter is a whore. And just consider, the milk on her lips is not yet dry".

I was curious about the Hunchback's daughter's behaviour, although less than about the story of her mother's demise, and it isn't at all surprising: the reigning beauty of an inhospitable shore marries a young, sickly man and a year after the birth of their first child unexpectedly dies – that would not leave anybody indifferent. Brooding on these memories of Jergi's mother, I unintentionally missed the end of this family argument. I soon understood, however, that I couldn't work anything out.

And when I shook myself, and tried to listen again, it was already too late – a seagull cawed – father and daughter had already drawn away into the distance. I too hurried home.

But I wanted to know more about Charlie's death than others did. For that, naturally I had to head to the billiard room. I met Mergen on the way. But he wasn't at all interested in hearing yet another version. In his opinion, it had happened like this: as evening approached, the boy had one too many, dived into the turbulent sea, and there the storm got him. I admit I found such warped judgement mildly irritating, and I tried to argue with him all over again in the half-empty billiard room. I asked how he explained the blood on the drowned boy's temple. It turned out that he didn't know anything about that little fact, but it was hard for him to give up his haughty attitude towards outsiders. You see, he was a local, and locals … there weren't that many of them here, while guys like Charlie, visitors, who are mainly remembered by locals as the drowned guys, he saw all the time. He had, therefore, a very peculiar relationship to them. You could put it like this: He doesn't find it particularly upsetting, but keeps count at least: what day and what time? The victim's age was recorded as well.He has no interest in any further details, and he was also wholly indifferent to my speculation about the blood on his temple, he said:

"Does a drunk guy smash against the rock for a long time? Thankfully, it was only a single blow this time," he said, not contemplating for a minute that the injury would hardly have been sustained in the water. It wouldn't have been so deep, and the blood would have been washed away by the water.

Aman didn't let me put forward my own version of Charlie's death. He said:

"A man can die anytime, and without any relation to his character or conduct. So, every now and then a living being perishes this way, unsuspectingly plunging to their death. And he was just unlucky, trapped in the jaws like a beast in a snare."

In this insulting, long-winded way, he summarized the tragedy of man. I don't know how the others were feeling, but his reasoning was close to my heart, only not in relation to the conditions of Charlie's death, but in an abstract sense, on its own.

On the fifth day, the drowned girl's body had still not yet surfaced, although according to those in the know it ought to have, and a lot sooner than, well, winter.

By that time, I had already almost drawn my inferences and conclusions as to the links between Charlie's death and his girlfriend, if of course, she was his girlfriend. Nevertheless, I did not rush to share my impressions with just anybody but preferred to listen to the observations of others.

On one of the subsequent uncommonly hot days, an equally heated argument broke out in the billiard room. I entered the thick of the discussion while Samed was speaking. He was Aman's rival, and therefore a number of spectators had gathered around the table. Everybody was waiting for something new from those arguing, not just recycled rumours.

"No!" Samed disagreed with one of the guys who flocked around the table. "It wasn't suicide!"

Awkwardly knocking the cue against a ball by the far side of the table, he argued with himself: "If I'm completely accurate, it was suicide, but only in a very specific sense of the word, the figurative, so to speak."

"What on earth are you talking about?" questioned his bemused interlocutor. "Was it suicide, or wasn't it?"

"Well it was like this. He was tipsy and went for a swim. I saw a woman with him - attractive, blonde. We bumped into each other under the lamplight. They were definitely going towards the sea. It was about 11 o'clock. Who on earth goes for a swim at that time? I even said, where are you going this late?"

"Wait, so, you asked them?"

"No, why? I asked myself that. If I'm honest about it, he himself is to blame. Cherchez la femme, as they say."

Ready to pot the next ball, Aman, as an aside, asked him:

"Are you saying he was drunk?"

"Between us, he didn't usually drink," countered Samed. "But it's obviously, what this is all about. Nobody simply dies like that."

"True enough," answered Aman distractedly, rounding off this comment with a decisive elegant shot. The ball leaped up, before landing smoothly in a pocket.

"Remember," Samed addressed the crowd of avid spectators, "remember, the year before last, one guy, the very same thing? They barely saved him. Actually, he had this really hot chick with him, guys. Oh, she was so beautiful!"

"Yes, there was that time," wearily answered one of them. "But he was an alchy, lord save us. But this one ... been drinking with someone, had he?"

Nobody answered the question. I too remained silent, even though I knew more than the rest of them. And there was one person among us who could have shown off with an answer. But it isn't the time for that.

Someone called for Samed outside. He said his goodbyes, gave the cue to Mergen, and went into the vestibule lined with fake palms in pots. Under the palms, an attractive blonde was waiting for him. We were all slightly at a loss, as Samed had left at the most interesting moment.

A silence descended. And only Aman fulfilled my wavering hope that the conversation would continue; he became suddenly enlivened, as if with the exit of Samed, the leader who had been instigating the argument, he had received the winner's garland. More intuitively, rather than relying on any sound logic, I guessed that Aman had still not yet come clean with everything he knew about Charlie's final days. But I just didn't understand the real motive for his protracted silence, not that day, in the billiard room, when he suddenly opened up, nor now, when that frightening tragedy, faded into the past, has already become clouded by the mist of time and on the verge of being forgotten completely.

"So this one time, I'm walking along the shore..."

He aimed at the far corner from an extremely comfortable position. He paused in his tale for just long enough to ready himself for the next shot.

"Right, so, I'm walking along the shore, if I remember, around ten days ago, then..." He hesitated. "Somewhere ... somewhere, yeah it must have been! Maybe five days before all of this. It was after dinner, naturally."

Aman worked in a small office, which carried out monitoring, incomprehensible to the majority of inhabitants here, of the local flora and fauna, and even of the atmosphere. Nobody was sure if the office really was a branch of some research institute in the capital, or if the sign concealed something else completely opposite to conservation of the surrounding environment. In addition to this, Aman himself now and again made allusions, and suggestively hinted at the particular singularity of his line of work. What is more, none of us had ever been inside the building.

But in the summertime, like now, Aman "went a-wooing" as he called his short-term dalliances with visiting beauties. Strange as it may seem, he always made an irresistible impression on the female sex, regardless of the fact that he was far from an Adonis. Obviously there was something beyond his modish wardrobe that just attracted and dazzled girls. In the moments when he was awash with feelings of kindness, you could talk to him about matters of the heart, and his hazel eyes would sparkle with a special light, making his face rather attractive. He completely transformed, and his large stomach seemed to recede, becoming less noticeable.

Having pocketed the ball, Aman took up a comfortable position, and finally continued:

"Right then, so I go along the shore and see Charlie, lying face down by the water, half-way in the water. Breathing heavily. I ask: 'What lad are you doing splashing around in the shallows?' He lifted his blackened face towards me, with a look in his eyes, I didn't get it, either a plea or fear -- in a word, wild. It made my stomach turn. I understood that it wasn't worth waiting for a response, but then he started to speak: 'You know... I've been there!' His speech was stilted. As he said these first words, he pointed behind him with a shaking hand, towards the sea:

"'Strange thing...I died. Right now, I'm already dead!'"

All of the people listening froze. Somebody gave a gasp, shocked by his last pronouncement. Aman, having adequately relished our reactions, leisurely continued, savouring every word.

"I crouched down. And stared him in the eye and understood that he wasn't lying. 'How did this happen?' I asked him. And then he confessed, 'I swam out far, farther than usual. It was surprisingly easy to swim. As if there was no water at all, and instead some air was carrying my body. At some point, I happened to turn around and saw that the shore was not behind me. It had disappeared! Transformed into a mist! Finally, I saw it, but it had taken a lot of strength to get there... and you could barely call it a shore, the thing I could see. It fluttered in the distance, as if it were an ethereal curtain: one minute visible, the next gone.'"

Aman set the cue down, wiped his sweaty hands with a towel, and coiled one end around his right hand. Everybody was nervous, but Aman more than us, so his speech became a little confused:

"I was listening closely to a guy who said, who - who... had only just escaped the clutches of death. You know, friends, how much I went through then, listening to him! Charlie was so worried, he, hi... his face was so, so completely, lifeless... so, you understand, it was as if I was chatting with a dead man!"

Aman hesitated for a second, but those listening were desperate to know the rest of the story. And somebody prodded the narrator:

"Aman, what happened next? What happened next?"

Aman frowned, and twitched nervously:

"Next...Charlie said that it was as if half the world had turned on him, his hands and feet were seized with..." Aman paused, trying to remember the word.

"Cramps?" prompted somebody.

"No, not cramps, something different! But I remember... fear, not fear, some kind of grief! Yes, that's it...he said: 'An inhuman grief has overcome me! And I am alone. I think, in any case, that I can't describe the absolute terror I experienced, you can't put that in words. I fought with the sea, and, it seems, I lost... There are many of us people, and we don't have time to think about true grief, for we live together only once. Is that not the source of our grief? Is that not the source of our unhappiness and future ruination?'"

Aman glanced at us and our devastation, and understood that he had achieved the desired effect. For a split second, I even seemed to see a vision. It was as if it was not Aman standing before us but the drowned boy himself, Charlie... It was he who reached out his hand from the depths of the sea and admonished us:

"We don't think deeply about the meaning of life. It's a shame. It would be worth it... within a few seconds, balanced between the sky and the sea, life and death, I learned more about the earthly essence of humanity, than all of my years so far. Me, I have had enough of that for a long time, maybe not only me... but... it doesn't matter anymore, but sure, fine... we are alone in this life... Alone in all the universe! Alone even on this earth, and the sea – is our enemy! Believe me, we have no friends in the entire universe save ourselves. That's what I learned, when I hung helplessly between the sky and the earth, choking on salt water... Yes, we are alone! But we won't understand that ever. And, possibly, humanity will commit suicide..."

In the billiard room, a deadly silence hung. It seemed none of us were even breathing. The silence became unbearable and, wanting to break it, I threw myself towards the door – to get away from there, to the open air, even if the heat is scorching, but to life, to shake myself free from the oppressive atmosphere.

Well, there you have it all. All there is to know about him, about Charlie.

The drowned girl's body was found that same evening, having finally been mercifully floated from the depths of the sea back to the living. We, a small group of witnesses, gathered in an oppressive silence around the body in a semicircle. Some official cars pulled up, out of which came police investigators and paramedics. Like automated beings, they carried out their usual work while we all stood and watched the girl, who just a few days ago had still been beautiful. Not long ago at all, she had still been alive, laughing, kissing, breathing...

She took leave of us in a hideous manner: one of the paramedics clumsily took her elbow, and the drowned girl, as if curtsying – or attempting to – sat up... that, in any case, is how it seemed to us. There was something significant in this last action.

I was restless throughout the night, almost without sleep. If for a short time I drifted off, then all at once I woke up, because my hand was being tugged at either by Charlie, or by the nameless girl-- as if they were asking me to pull them from the abyss. Having slept terribly, and without breakfast, I went out to the sea. It seemed to be in a calm state of bliss, innocently throwing an azure eye towards the sky. This, after everything it has done?

So now I am sitting on the bank and thinking about all that has happened. And wondering whether I have understood the full import of Charlie's words as I should? Maybe, but I doubt it.

It's possible I managed to gather some specks of truth or to add some strokes to the non-existent portrait. But the most important thing, the secret thing, maybe, slips away as always, and remains unfathomable. Maybe, it was after he felt this strange loneliness, and was faced for the smallest of moments by the secret of human existence, that Charlie a few days before his mysterious, grotesque death called me to share a modest feast in a tent during the midday heat. And merrily, laughing without a care, raised a glass of scarlet wine.

LOVE IN LILAC

Translated by Lois Kapila

The sun rose higher and in the lilac garden everything was painfully familiar. Arslan had only to close his eyes and he felt like he was far away, at home in Ashgabat. Back when he had been a schoolboy there, he had loved to wander amongst the lilac bushes in early spring. He had always adored their powerful scent and would sit at times for hours on some secluded bench until his head spun from the intoxicating smell and he would leave the garden, staggering. Even now, he should have left long ago but he lingered, eyes closed, lost in distant dreams. He simply didn't have the strength to get up and walk home to the hostel. Just the very thought of all the books waiting there to be read was enough to make him crazy. Summer exams were just around the corner and he just sat there, daydreaming about some far-off place as if waiting for some secret adventure to start.

It was spring, after all. Arslan sat contentedly, casually glancing at the occasional passers-by, and listening to the birds' chirping as they fluttered around. A flourish of fragrant lilac swayed above his head. Here and there a few, light wisps of white clouds floated across the lofty sky. It was so clear overhead that the dome of the sky seemed totally transparent, illusionary and infinite. The rich trill of a nightingale drifted from a thicket of leafy trees. It would soon be summer. In Ashgabat, the lilacs must have already blossomed but there was no way he would get to wander down his street there this year and luxuriate in their scent.

The edge of the lilac garden was next to his home by an old, brick building where – until recently – a girl about his age named Leila had lived. Further on, the garden gently tumbled beyond a low wooden fence and disappeared into the depths of the yard. How badly he wanted to meet Leila this spring in the lilac garden, although she might still think of him as the annoying kid who had never missed the chance to pull her pigtails. Wasn't that why she had thought he was a bully and had kept her distance when they'd run into each other? Until she'd moved to the other end of the town, that is. Maybe he was the reason Leila's parents had decided to move away from that street, which was a shame because he had liked her a lot. He just hadn't known for a long time how to act around her, so he'd done all kinds of stupid stuff.

It was sad. Arslan closed his eyes.

When he opened them, he saw that a girl he didn't recognize had appeared at the other end of the bench, as if by magic. This beautiful, fair-skinned girl sat quietly, reading. She looked about two years older than him. Arslan decided she was a student. Why else would she waste a marvellous spring day reading, especially now, when everything around them sang with poetry?

Arslan gave a little cough to try to attract her attention, but nothing happened. She was quite absorbed in her reading. He tried to guess who she was. She looked much like all the other students, but there was something peculiar about her. I wonder what she's reading about, thought Arslan. Perhaps about love?

He continued to watch this stranger, following the expressions on her face and her movements, and came to the conclusion from her demeanour that she was holding either a book of poetry or a novel about love. After all, can you really read about anything else while sitting amongst blossoming lilacs in a Moscow garden in May?

The girl was completely absorbed in her book and Arslan decided she hadn't even noticed him when she'd sat down on the bench. What a girl, he marvelled, and what hair! He closed his eyes again, not wanting his attention to unnerve the girl in case, God forbid, she should suddenly fly away. He didn't want her to disappear. On the contrary, he wanted her to stay there a bit longer – out of reach, perhaps, but near.

More time passed and Arslan became lost in daydreams again. But soon his thoughts drifted back to the stranger. If we knew each other, he thought, we could go together right now to the look-out point on top of Sparrow Hills or down to the Moskva River and get lost there by the water, in the Singing Forest, and in the evening we could go out to the cinema together. But it's not bad in the lilac garden, either, especially as evening draws in.

He imagined them walking there among the tall, fragrant lilac bushes, embracing like real lovers. They would even kiss, maybe, as the light fades and the red disk of the sun grows large, then disappears over the Western horizon, leaving behind the scent of datura in the evening air. That same potent datura which makes the girls' heads spin. He had heard just the other day how a student for no apparent reason had lost consciousness here in the garden. A crowd had quickly gathered around her and somebody had called an ambulance. But when it arrived the medics had to search all of the benches for the patient and when they had found her, they didn't know how to react – whether to be livid or to laugh. She was already passionately kissing a guy, just like all the other couples in the area. The doctor and the nurse discreetly gathered some sprigs of lilac, made their own intoxicating posy and went on their way, laughing good-naturedly about the emergency call for a patient diagnosed as "love-struck".

***

This summer, Arslan felt like a grown-up. He dreamt of girls more and more, and, curiously, they slipped into his dreams as they would into the sea, completely naked. He couldn't wait to experience real, grown-up love. But it was unlikely to happen now, before exams, with so little time. Yet the aroma of the lilac garden lingered in the air, beckoning with ever more force, rousing ever more deeply, his pure, youthful desires.

***

The sun was fiery hot but Arslan didn't want to move to the shade, and didn't want to open his eyes. He was scared that the enchanting stranger might no longer be beside him. So he stayed there until the heat became unbearable, and only then did he open his eyes. He was surprised to see the stranger hadn't vanished. Rather, she had made herself more comfortable by taking off her shoes and tucking up her feet, exactly like the women in his distant homeland. And what legs she had, visible under her skirt. What dainty ankles. Arslan could hear his heart beating. He could no longer act indifferently. He wanted to talk to the girl.

And, of course, without giving it much thought, he asked her the first question that came into his head.

"Aren't you hot, Miss? Are you sure you're not going to get sunburnt by mistake?"

The girl looked up and smiled at him, and answered cheerfully, "By mistake, no, but maybe on po-o-rpose."

Arslan also gave an unwitting smile, but more at her pronunciation than her words. That's interesting, thought the curious boy. Which republic is she from? Maybe one of the Baltics? Must be one of the Baltics. Where else would she get an accent like that?

"Where are you from, Miss?" he asked. And then started to try to guess: Riga? No. Tallinn? No. Lithuania?

"I'm from Sveeden."

Arslan was confused by her answer. "Ho-ow?" he asked, warily. "Just like that? Straight from Sweden?"

The girl gave him that sweet smile which, later, over the following days and weeks, would appear so often in his dreams at night.

"Yes, and so vat? I'm from Stockholm."

"But how did you get there … to Stockholm? You've, what, lived there all your life?" The words unwittingly escaped from Arslan's mouth.

"I'm Sveedish," she answered, with a giggle.

Arslan was at a bit of a loss. He had no idea how to act now, what to say to her. Should he carry on the conversation, or should he excuse himself and slip away? He was even ready to close his eyes again but curiosity got the better of him. He couldn't keep from looking at his enchanting neighbour. He started to speak again, but his words came out all muddled:

"But you, it's the very, truly, are you, I mean Swedish? Right from there?" he mumbled, glancing around with a confused look. "It's the first time in my whole life I've seen a real-life Swedish girl. How did you end up here? I mean, are you a student, or have you come to visit, to see Moscow?"

"I came for an internshe-e-p for a co-o-ple of months. I speak Russian wery badly."

"No, what are you talking about?" Arslan hurried to encourage her. "You speak very well, amazingly even! You're not Russian, after all. Sure, it's a little funny but also sweet. I like it."

"Do-o you?" the Swedish girl smiled sincerely. "Probably, you're yust light-headed from the smell of the lilac."

"Yes," Arslan confessed dreamily, glancing at the lilac bushes. "It's insanely beautiful and fragrant here. But, I'm probably more flustered because it's the first time I've had a conversation with such a beautiful girl." And then, having slowed down a little, added, "with a Swedish girl."

"Vat, so every Svedish girl you have met so var has been ugly?"

"No, no, I didn't mean that!" Arslan hurried to reassure her. "They all were very beautiful, very sweet. What's more, I haven't seen them yet, that is, I've seen them, but not like you, right next to me, but at the cinema, on the television and, you know, in various pretty magazines."

He turned a deep red, both from his secret thoughts and from the sudden, fleeting memory of those pictures he had seen in the glossy magazines. They were passed around now and then, spending no more than one night with each person, as if they weren't pictures, but real-life girls in gilded cages.

"I understaa-and," drawled his companion, as if she'd guessed the reason for his embarrassment, and started to laugh. "So you lo-o-ve Svedish girls in magazines!"

"Yes, very much," confessed Arslan, a bit unsure of himself. "Life abroad is so interesting: the weather, nature, how people dress and, all in all, what things are like. I've not been, of course, and I know that I don't know anything about you."

"Vat's your name?" asked the Swedish girl.

"Arslan. And yours?"

"Bibi," she answered. When he heard that, Arslan almost fell off the bench.

"Ho-ow's that? Bibi? So, they call you Bibi? Well we've got that name, too. It's even really popular. You could say there are Bibis on every street. I had a classmate called Bibi!"

"That's nice. Ve call Bridgettes, Bibi. It's easier, and quicker too. But Arslan – that's a Russian name?"

"No, in Russian it would be Lev," and just to be on the safe side he started to growl. "Rrrrr!.. You get it. Lion, kind of big and hairy, and strong, too!"

"You're frightening me." She closed the book, getting up from the bench.

She's not kidding, Arslan thought, alarmed. She's leaving. He made a desperate suggestion:

"Don't you want to take a walk? It's so lovely here. It's not going to last long. The lilacs in Moscow pass quickly. By this time last year, they were already gone. Spring's come a bit later this time. You could say you've been fabulously lucky."

"I'm re-e-lly glad. Let's go, then. But if ve go for a valk together, you're not allowed to eat me like a lion, okay?"

Arslan was at a loss and, unable to come up with a response straightaway. He glanced at his companion carefully, trying to understand if she was joking or serious. Flustered, he again muttered something silly, completely off the mark, which as soon as he said it seemed funny even to him.

"No, don't get me wrong, I don't each much meat, I prefer fish. They just call me Arslan, but I'm practically vegetarian. What's more ... how to put it ... I'm soon going to be a bit busy, I need to wash my trousers, shirt, otherwise I'll have nothing to wear to school."

"You, vat, still go to school? But you are old!"

Her remark struck Arslan to the core. He laughed out loud. But at the same time, he became a touch ashamed of his words, of his anxiety, perhaps, in front of this enchanting foreign girl.

"No, I mean, when we're talking amongst ourselves, we call our university 'school'. You don't do that?"

And from that moment, one thing led to another, and they were quickly drawn into a conversation of "in your country, in our country" and didn't even notice they had been walking around the garden almost arm in arm.

Bibi asked him. "Vat's dat scar on your cheek?"

He joked, "I had this scrap with a real tiger."

"Va-at? With a real one?" she said, scared. "And you're still alive? But, where does the tiger live now? He's alive?"

"I think he's alive although I'm not sure. I was lucky that I'm a leo, otherwise that could have ended in tears." Arslan pulled a mournful expression, but then, laughing, added, "Then again, it's possible that without crying, you won't get anywhere in any case, since I was a rather young boy then, just a child in nappies, when this predator, tiger of a sandfly attacked me."

But then, seeing Bibi's blank look, he said, "It's a *pendinka*, a mark from the bite of a sandfly, which you get in our part of the world."

"Pendin? Sandfly? Vat's that?" Bibi couldn't understand.

So Arslan set about explaining the meaning of these words. From that moment, he adopted the role of teacher with delight. The walk in the lilac garden was a revelation for Arslan. He had never thought, never guessed, that you could have such an interesting conversation with a foreign girl on a first meeting. By the end of the walk, mind you, he had already forgotten that Bibi was Swedish and started to consider her accent normal. When they parted, they agreed to meet again the next day after lectures, in the same place in the garden. It's worth hurrying to enjoy a lilac fairy tale. It doesn't last long, after all.

As he fell asleep in his little room in the hostel, Arslan smiled at the thought of Bibi, her slim waist, her white wrists, the tender radiance of her heavenly eyes. And the way she looked at him. Trustingly, as if they had known each other forever and as if he were older than her, and not the other way around. It was the first time he had felt this. He'd been confident, sitting alone with a girl. That feeling of self-satisfaction boosted his ego. For a long time he couldn't fall asleep, and he trembled gently as if waves were rolling over him. In his mind, memories stirred of the fleeting touches of Bibi's delicate fingers, and the smell of the lilac bushes lulled him to sleep.

He met her every day after lectures and on Sundays they simply never left each other's sides. Arslan's head was spinning. Bibi exuded the sweetness of May. Everything to do with the enchanting Swedish girl was bathed in a tender, lilac haze. In the evenings, Arslan brought lush bouquets from the university garden to her room in secret. They gave off a perfume of both the night air of Moscow at the onset of summer, and of the beguiling datura, for he gathered the bouquets for Bibi while the love trills of the nightingales drifted from the deep-scented bushes.

Bibi really liked to walk with him in the evenings to the look-out point to admire the bird's-eye view of golden-domed Moscow. Arslan was proud of "this beauty," as he would call Moscow, the capital of his vast homeland. He would talk with enthusiasm about this maddening city, but he preferred to go with her to the cinema, and on the way back explain the definitions of Russian words, just like he had the first day they had met. He liked to sit up late in some cosy little café and go back home on the crowded night bus, forced to stand, pressed up close to each other. Arslan was glad of the compulsory intimacy. Their happy faces were reflected in the bus windows, and it seemed as if their feelings were printed there, frozen symbols of their love that floated onwards, leaving behind the sleepy, nocturnal streets of the city.

The route from the bus stop to the hostel always ran through the university garden and they would stay there until midnight. Short, tender kisses gave way to passionate, lingering ones. Arslan already remembered their first kiss as if it had happened in the distant past, even though it had been just a few days earlier. He felt like he had grown up. And the world, too, seemed to him more grown-up, unspeakably beautiful, marked by motherly devotion and feminine gentleness. Day and night, his young soul was filled with love and unexpressed tender feelings. He worshipped Bibi so much that when she told him he kissed passionately and with skill, he felt drunk from this female praise.

He became at once smiley and serious, careful and forgetful, sociable and reserved. It was impossible not to see. And, of course, it was his classmates who first noticed these dramatic changes.

"You're getting all grown-up!" said Olga with a friendly smile, looking at him intently. Mind you, she was always looking at him in a special way, Arslan knew. And now she looked deeply into his sparkling eyes.

"Why's that? Probably spring is taking its toll? In Ashgabat, it's time for you to get married," she joked. "But you're spending all your time wandering in the lilac garden, oblivious to everybody around you."

"I'll find myself a bride here. There's no need to go to Ashgabat!" he answered, unexpectedly assertive. But then he frowned a little. How did she know about his meetings with Bibi in the lilac garden? Had she been spying on him?

That day it seemed to him that both the class *Komsorg*[1] and the *Partorg* were watching him out of the corners of their eyes. The latter more than once gave him a stern, openly disapproving look, without saying a word. Although he felt he really wanted to, or had to, say something. It was then that Arslan remembered for the first time in recent days one of the unwritten rules of the Moscow State University, which he had recalled at the very start of his acquaintance with Bibi but had later somehow forgotten. He had known earlier that to get tangled up with foreigners was "not recommended" and that there were no exceptions. How on earth could he have forgotten? This was bad. What was he supposed to do? Now he knew what the *Komsorg* and *Partorg's* sidelong glances signified, and also those stern looks from the warden, who sat outside the entrance to Bibi's halls where, for the most part, the foreigners lived. He had read whatever he wanted into those glances, but never reproach.

He suddenly felt worried and uneasy. He knew he'd accidentally crossed an invisible line and felt depressed. He wasn't himself for the rest of the lesson but when the lecture ended he hurried to meet Bibi, as if his worries had never existed. That's how everything continued, as normal: during the

---

1   The Komsorg, Partorg and Proforg (see lower) were all unpaid grassroots-level functionaries who worked in universities and institutes during the Soviet Union. The terms stand for Komsomol leader, party organiser and trade union leader, respectively.

day, he was tormented by suspicious glances but, later, he forgot them. Just consider that, with all those *Komsorgs*, and *Proforgs*, and *Partorgs*. He was in love. His heart was full of lilac love.

No sooner had he stepped outside the walls of the old university building, which sat snugly on Karl Marx Avenue in the heart of Moscow, than Arslan hurried as if nothing had happened to meet his captivating Scandinavian sweetheart. The glances of "all those guys" became sterner each day, more meaningful and eloquent. Arslan chased away any sinister thoughts with sheer will power. He desperately wanted to distance himself from their hostility and so, as soon as he left the faculty, he deliberately forgot about his silent stalkers. But his ill-wishers wouldn't leave him in peace. The course *Partorg*, who paraded around in a long, leather coat in both winter and summer, "accidentally" bumped into him at the door of the Lenin Auditorium, and said in an angry voice, "Lad, stop with this silliness, because I really don't feel like hearing all kinds of unflattering nonsense about you."

"What silliness?" asked Arslan, not immediately grasping the sharply spoken words.

"You know, what!" In three words, the *Partorg* sliced though the young man's hardness of hearing and, pointedly turning his back without saying another word, he walked away.

That same evening, the warden in the part of the hostel where Bibi lived, apparently having forgotten about the bell, began to beat angrily with her gnarled knuckles on the door and, when the young boy stuck his nose out of the room, gave him a piece of her mind about the systematic violation of the internal code of conduct. Trying to spot a violation over his shoulder, she crabbily ordered Arslan to leave the foreign girl's room right that minute and get back to his own. The route between zones (she enthusiastically called the areas of the hostel "zones") was blocked at exactly twenty-three hundred hours, she pointed out, and he risked getting locked out. And what's more, she said, because of him, she might get a talking to.

"Young man, it'th jutht not fair at the end of the day!" lisped and mumbled the old Ukrainian woman through her metal row of front teeth. "I don't want to be booted out of my job at my age. Have a heart."

The next day, though, it finally happened just as it should. Bibi and he became closer – a lot closer – than before. When *that* happened the well-brought-up, principled boy, began to think about a swift marriage. He lay for a long time with his eyes closed, his mind travelling through a montage of the future, which was full of colourful episodes. He imagined how, arm in arm with Bibi, he would appear at home in Ashgabat to introduce her to his parents.

"We have to get up ... the babushka is coming. She'll get angry, you know," Bibi said almost wordlessly, with just one movement of her lips.

They went out to the garden but it was difficult to part so they took a little stroll, intoxicated by their new, nocturnal happiness. It seemed that the lilac gave off an even stronger, sweeter aroma than before.

"How warm and cosy! Now it's not even cold at night," exclaimed Arslan, but then a sudden sadness welled up from nowhere. "It's June. The lilacs are almost over. We haven't long left to enjoy them."

Their lips melted furtively into a long and passionate kiss, which seemed to contain within it a tremor of concern for their future but they hadn't yet guessed that the lilac garden would never greet them, as a couple, again. The kiss became bitter, or did it just seem bitter to Arslan?

***

He was picked up by the KGB with a sickening lack of ceremony.

When they came for him, he hadn't had time to wake up properly after the late night.

The bell had just rung, the professor had just walked into the auditorium, and started to spread out his papers on his lecture table, sleepily mumbling the usual ritual phrases. The students had just settled down at their desks, and at that very minute the door quietly opened to the Lenin Auditorium, where about two hundred future journalists were either snatching clandestine bites of their morning sandwiches or sitting wide-eyed and lost in daydreams. Many thought it was one of the latecomers rushing in after the professor so that, having darted in unnoticed, they could quickly sit down somewhere in the first row – with the most industrious of the industrious students.

But they were wrong. It wasn't a latecomer. Arslan was called out of the room.

He went out and, right outside the door, saw an unfamiliar, young man in a foppish, checked suit. The visitor, who kept straightening his tie, made sure to look closely at Arslan, as if memorizing his appearance.

"So can I go now?" begged the faculty administrator, Valentina Yermolayevna, in an unusually timid voice, her tone alerting Arslan that the young man in the somewhat frivolous suit was no ordinary visitor and that he, Arslan, was in a tough spot. Possibly a very bad one indeed. That was also clear from the woman's deep sigh.

"Yes, of course!" answered the young man, in an especially polite tone. "We will now just… deal with this on our own, isn't that right, Arslan?"

Arslan was perplexed and stayed silent, but Valentina Yermolayevna, demonstrating complete obedience and also, apparently, having no part in what was happening, quickly retreated, leaving the fate of her student wholly in the hands of the guest.

It was the first time Arslan had seen the faculty administrator so bewildered, almost helpless, and the first time that she had looked at him with such deep fear in her faintly reddish, slightly bulging eyes, and his heart immediately sank. When he heard the solemn order, "Follow me and bring your things with you," he went back to the auditorium and under the crossfire of his course mates' eyes, clumsily gathered up his textbooks and notepads and then, head hanging, dejected, silently plodded out to the street, noticing only the soles of the pretty shoes on the warden's feet.

A car stood on the edge of a narrow side-street, which by an ironic twist of fate, was named after one of the most freedom-loving rebel writers of national literature, Herzen.

"Right, young man, let's go to our office. It's not far from here," said his companion, sitting in the car and appearing disinterested, but keeping a close eye on Arslan's movements.

It felt like the car hadn't even had time to pull away, they arrived so quickly. An enormous grey building seemed to swallow them for breakfast, cutting off any way out. They walked for a long time through a labyrinth of corridors, down stairs, and back up, and then back down again, between the floors. Those who they passed briskly greeted Arslan's companion. If he hadn't known about the KGB, hadn't known where they'd taken him, then he could have preserved a normal, merry mood. But now it was way beyond that. Inside the grey building everybody looked unusually busy. Markedly polite people noiselessly floated down the corridors, nipping from office to office, all with identical folders either tucked under their arms or clutched to their chests. The whole time, they never met a person with empty hands. Arslan thought: they really love their documents.

Finally, his companion slowed down, stopped opposite one of the offices and rapped on the enormous door.

"Yes?" a curt voice said from inside the room. "Come in!"

"Comrade colonel, from *Zhurfak*[2] ..."

"You can enter!" came the muffled answer from the owner of the office, a man around fifty years old, who was sitting and intently writing something. And, as Arslan later remembered with distress, he only glanced at him for a fraction of a second. What's more, Arslan wasn't even sure that he noticed him. Maybe, he didn't see him at all? His gaze just skipped over Arslan, like when people accidentally bump into each other at the door of a public toilet. His escort quickly retreated, after indicating with a finger where to sit, and the colonel once again became busy with his papers, which were brightly lit by a splash of light from a dark table lamp, the strange shape of which surprised Arslan. Something from the Middle Ages, the student couldn't help but think.

In the office, there was complete silence. Arslan, expecting questions, at first just sat there, breathing in and out, in and out. The silence didn't get to him at first. For a while, he was still thinking maybe they'd brought him to the colonel at a very lucky time. After all, it was clear he was way too busy to deal with him. But, with time, the silence became more conspicuous and then even more oppressive. The colonel was clearly writing something, maybe even some kind of report, because Arslan had to wait a lot longer than he had expected.

For the first few minutes, he was glad that he hadn't been leapt on straightaway; it gave him time to catch his breath from the journey. Although, he didn't understand why he should be leapt at, since he didn't feel guilty at all. Maybe that was why he began to brace himself for something unknown, like for an exam, getting ready to respond to any question in a clear and concise manner and, of course, with dignity, just as Tuchborskaya, their professor for foreign literature had taught them. He didn't understand why they had brought him to this gloomy place, why they had dragged him from his lecture right before the start of the summer exams. That the reason could have been his love for Bibi, he didn't even want to consider.

He realized he had a bit of time to think about it all, and he frantically began to wonder what had happened, why he was there. Sure, he had committed a few small sins: scrapped with a friend back home, called him a cheapskate; argued in a shop with the saleswoman when she short-changed him. But he hadn't even argued with her that rudely, he hadn't used a single swear word – and not because he didn't know such words, but simply

---

2   Faculty of Journalism

because he believed it would be unbecoming for a future journalist to use improper phrases. After he found nothing in the recent past, he plunged further back, sifting through his youth, then his distant childhood. There was plenty of time. The colonel continued to scribble; he evidently hadn't got to him yet. He was writing, stooped over the desk. That is a bad habit, thought Arslan. It will quickly make you a hunchback, or maybe it already has. He couldn't tell for sure, as the writer still hadn't got up from his desk. If he becomes a hunchback, thought Arslan, then his wife won't love him any more ...

And then it dawned on him. Could they have brought him here because of love? He didn't want to believe it, it would be too absurd. So, after a moment, he began to rummage about in his memory in search of more plausible reasons for being brought to the grey building, which was by no means a popular place amongst future journalists. And for that matter probably also amongst physicists and chemists, linguists and biologists, and students from other faculties.

He delved into his memory, remembering everything that had happened over the last few days, then the last few months, and then the last few years. But it seemed there was nothing more serious than his love for a foreign girl. There were, of course, scuffles in the yard, and his father's cigarettes – borrowed, naturally, without asking – and a few episodes from his teenage years, even a few quite turbulent ones, but young lads' stuff all the same. Nobody could seriously be interested in any of that, especially not the staff at an institution like this.

He even cheered up a bit, finally convinced that, for all intents and purposes, he had nothing to fear from this close-lipped colonel. During the first two or three hours, Arslan tried to maintain this sense of confidence. After all, that was the only protection he had. And with the glimmer of that possibility, he could distance himself a bit from his completely understandable, human concerns. But he couldn't shake that torturous feeling that there was something he didn't know and, as time passed, his initial fighting spirit began to wane.

The colonel remained silent, as if secretly laughing at how he'd left the student to torment himself, without any help, ever more mercilessly, more severely. Arslan again and again dug through his past, which at first glance had turned out to be not that special or eventful, and searched for some awkward moments, and the longer he dwelt on them, the more clearly he saw that they were no help at all.

So he began to make them up in his imagination and soon began to believe something had happened that he had forgotten but the colonel knew about. He was vaguely aware he was inventing complete nonsense but it was difficult to stop: he sank deeper into the wilds of his own conscience, where he became frightened. Finally, he came to the conclusion that the most dangerous of these suddenly "resurgent" memories was how he had compared his own battered cap to the cap of Lenin himself.

It happened during a class trip to a collective farm to pick potatoes when, after a long journey, all the students were hungry. Dinner was late as usual so Arslan dared joke that "even Lenin in the tsar's prison was better fed than us lot here, in the collective farm fields. After all, the chief used to write love letters every day to Nadezhda Konstantinovna in milk! And he had ink-pots made from black bread. And if you consider the fact that, by his own admission, he had to eat up a certain number of milky ink-pots every day as a precaution, and that, as everyone knows, is in addition to the prison grub, then there's no way you can compare these collective farm rations with Comrade Lenin's square meals!" Everybody had found his rambling joke funny, but then again Arslan had been among friends. But now ...

He wondered, what if the KGB colonel guessed what anti-Soviet jokes he had running through his head. So many! He could get a serious punishment for that. So he prayed to God for a rather long time to ask that the KGB guy couldn't pry into his thoughts and his memories of those *kolkhoz* wisecracks. He tried desperately to squeeze this sedition – which he, in essence, had brought up in the first place – back deeper into himself, to stop it spilling out.

But then he started to feel painfully hungry and gradually thoughts of food forced out all others. A few hours later, this hunger somehow dulled and was instead replaced with thirst. He felt like he was in the hot, waterless Karakum Desert. Alone. Without a drop of water anywhere. He was about to fall off his chair from thirst. His lips became dry and he tried in vain to force out just a drop of saliva to moisten his lips, which had been numb since morning.

He struggled with his scratchy tongue and throat for quite a long time, before another infliction took their place – he really needed to go to the bathroom. The hours since morning had crept by like a long serpent, longer than the corridor they had walked down to get to this room which Arslan had already grown to despise, to this office of absolute silence.

From this moment, he no longer had any desires left, except those which come completely naturally. And during all of that unthinkably long stretch of time, the KGB colonel didn't even glance at him. He'd undoubtedly forgotten about Arslan.

For several hours, the colonel didn't react once to the fact that there was another living soul in the office besides himself. He just carried on writing and writing, sometimes pausing for a few phone calls, before settling down again to his business, scribbling line after line. From time to time, some papers were brought into the office and he signed them or, if he refused, he would softly, very softly, explain why he wouldn't do that and send them back for revision. Arslan was surprised at how he managed to speak so quietly yet so clearly, so that all his colleagues could do was nod their heads in agreement and then take back with them whatever they had brought. Only once did Arslan catch his exact words. It was when one of his subordinates, to support an argument he was making, used the already fashionable word *perestroika*. The colonel flew into a quiet rage, answering rather sharply, "We've all lived through a lot in our lifetime. We'll live through this, too. If worse comes to worst, the name will change, but it won't go further than that. *We* won't let it."

And right then, Arslan felt a growing fear, an unfamiliar fear of this sullen colonel and his silent power over others. He had heard from older generations that in this building they never bothered to stand on ceremony with their victims. During Stalin's times, people used to throw themselves out of the window of this gloomy building, unable to bear the cruel torture and suffering. Such memories obviously did nothing to revive his spirits.

It had been at least five hours since Arslan had been brought in, but the colonel continued as he always had, not deigning to give him even a glance. This contemptuous indifference had already become a form of torture. The young man sometimes felt the colonel's stony eyes on him but, no matter how hard he tried, he couldn't catch that moment. A quiet fear, as quiet as the voice of the colonel, grew out of this uncertainty. It gradually took hold of his soul and body. His heart also felt trapped, as it beat in his cage-like chest, painfully, aggrieved: what awaited him here, at the end of the day? What was this tireless colonel writing, sitting behind his enormous dark-brown table in this quiet, dimly lit office? There were no answers to any of these conceivable or inconceivable questions. And the colonel just carried on working.

He worked for so long that Arslan lost his urge to eat, was no longer tormented by thirst, and had just one desire left, which he just couldn't get rid of. He wanted to ask to go to the toilet but didn't dare. His fear of the colonel had grown many times over since he'd arrived. He started to understand that he was sitting there for a reason. It appeared his fate was being decided, if not in this office then somewhere deep within this building. So he forced himself to tolerate a hundred times more than a simple mortal could. At first his legs went numb, then his hands, and that numbness rose ever higher and higher, creeping towards his heart.

The colonel just carried on writing and writing, and there weren't any signs that his scribbling would stop in the foreseeable future. And Arslan tolerated it all, hoping that the colonel had to finish writing and, finally, begin to talk to him. When that happened, he wouldn't miss the opportunity to ask about his "need". But for the time being, he tolerated it, believing that he had no other way out. He was scared that if he asked, they could send him somewhere far away, forever. Maybe they provoke people just so they can then punish them in the most brutal way? They wouldn't catch him out that way! He'd die, but wouldn't give them the opportunity to deal with him so easily. They shouldn't try to break me, they've got no right! He still naively hoped that fate would somehow ease his suffering. It makes me wonder, Arslan thought. What's he really like? He's also human after all? How can he keep going? Why can't I tolerate this, while he willingly tolerates it?

Time passed but Arslan was already outside time. Then something unimaginable started to happen to the boy. His tongue gradually went numb. His ears popped. Not a single sound could reach Arslan. The colonel continued to work just as intensely as if it were early morning, but Arslan, it seemed, could no longer take any interest in time, which he could physically feel trickling through his body like water through sand while the other time, the time that existed for everybody and acted somewhere beyond the walls of this building, did not seem to concern him at all. He tried to imagine what his course mates were doing right now but he couldn't, the grey mass of human faces drowned in the impenetrable silence which made him feel sick inside.

A feeling of nausea swelled inside him, the desire to retch crept up his throat, but he painfully suppressed it. In an instant, his fright gave way to hatred, and a thought flashed through his head: they wanted to kill him, wanted him to die of a ruptured bladder. He looked entreatingly one last time at the colonel, who didn't think to pay him any attention and continued to sit and calmly write, taking no notice of Arslan, a living boy whom he obviously didn't want to see. The colonel was there and at the same time he wasn't. It was then that Arslan settled on a desperate plan.

At first, he didn't manage to do anything. He couldn't squeeze out a single drop, his own body had ceased to obey him, it was totally numb. He used his last bit of strength to fight himself, having altogether blocked out the tormentor-colonel and the office of torture. The fight with his own body lasted some time. He didn't know how long but, finally, a hot stream began to flow down his thigh, it seemed to come from right under his heart, drenching the chair. It flowed for a long time, but he couldn't and didn't want to stop. Arslan was overjoyed, he'd done it! He'd dared! Even if he hadn't managed to do anything else, at least he'd done that. Let them kill him now, but at least he hadn't let them kill him in that inhumane way.

He soundlessly breathed out and glanced at the colonel but met with a bent silhouette. After some more time passed, he started to hear a few sounds – the rustling of papers reached him, then a few more, and he felt his yellow veil, his dimmed eyes, begin to lighten. Arslan pointed the tip of his tongue out into the air, convinced that his tongue had begun to come back to life. He couldn't get enough of it, although he wasn't certain that his tongue would be of use to him any time soon. He continued to just sit there, until his trousers had at least partially dried on him. He wondered whether what he'd done had been childish, but what was done was done.

There was no clock on the wall, and none ticking anywhere nearby. It was tough without a clock. And on top of that, the office door hadn't opened for a long time. Arslan vaguely guessed that the work day had ended two, or maybe even five, hours earlier. Now, it must already be night time? But how could he find out when the only window in the colonel's office was covered by thick curtains. Finally, he had the gall to stand up and, as if in a dream, unsteadily moved towards the window. Lifting the edge of the heavy curtains, he looked out and saw darkness. It seemed strange. He wondered, with horror, if he'd gone blind. He wanted to see something other than a shadowy gloom. The darkness slowly started to retreat, but he couldn't work out which direction the window was facing. What he could see didn't resemble a familiar town. Everything was different and cold. He stood on his tiptoes, straining all of his exhausted body and opened his tired eyes wide, in order to find some familiar features in the sliver of life through the window.

And suddenly, right at the same moment as he had drawn himself up to his full height like a thin string, the colonel's icy voice struck at his back like a blade.

"Can you see Magadan[3] from the window?"

"N-oo," Arslan stammered with fear, startled, and drawing in a short gulp of air.

"Well you'll definitely see it, if you ever set eyes on your foreign girl again! Now get out of here."

He added, ill-temperedly: "Take your stool out in the corridor!" The colonel lifted his hefty chin in the direction of the chair on which Arslan had sat the whole day and whole evening. "Leave it there, in the corridor, I've still got work to do here. Get out of here... Romeo ..."

***

Arslan left the building devastated. He couldn't remember the route he had taken that morning, its corridors, steps and turns. The building itself just spat him out to "freedom," having carefully chewed him up in preparation and sucked out his zest for life.

The town deafened Arslan with the boom and clamour of its usual, frantic rhythm, as if trying to draw him back to normal life. It blinded the young man with countless billboards, emblazoned with enticing names – look, it's life! Come back, breathe, live!

But it wasn't easy to return to normal life. Arslan felt like it was all far away from him now. He felt detached from everything around him. Everything he saw every day and which had made him so happy was beyond him, behind him, not with him.

And the people hurrying by, and the cars rushing along the evening avenues, looked unreal, like playthings. Or was it he, Arslan, who had become a plaything?

He got onto the metro and, avoiding the few passengers onboard, tucked himself into the corner of an almost empty carriage and shut his eyes. He got off the metro far from the centre of town, at Universitetskaya

---

3   Hundreds of thousands of political prisoners or "enemies of the people" were sent to Magadan in Stalinist times. In isolated north-east Russia, the port-town served as a major transit centre from which people were sent to brutal forced-labour camps in the area.

Station, a stone's throw from the hostel. He stood undecided, still not quite believing he was free, and heaved a deep sigh. He couldn't avoid the path through the lilac garden. In the light of the evening street lamps, the withering lilac bushes appeared dejected, and their colour had become somehow unnatural, sickly. The familiar bench on which he had met Bibi, three weeks earlier, lay abandoned, hidden in the undergrowth. She wasn't in the garden. Perhaps she hadn't come, or perhaps she hadn't wanted to wait for him and had gone. He didn't want to consider the possibility that her study programme had ended earlier than his term, or that Bibi had already left town.

He dropped onto the bench that had once been his favourite, secretly hoping for some kind of miracle that would show him that everything he'd been through that day had been only a silly dream, nothing more, and that all he had to do was wake up, and everything would be back in place, everything would be like before. After all, all it would take to return to life would be for Bibi to appear, here, now. But at the same time, he was hopelessly aware deep down that it was already impossible.

So he slowly got up and, reeling from tiredness, went back to his room, to the hostel.

***

And the night wind, and the scent of the last, wilting lilac bushes chased after him in vain, trying to stop him, to rouse his memory, to get him to turn back. It was the same caressing, summer wind, but with each step he took it was overpowered, again and again, by the sharp scent of urine, which chased away any memories of those recent days.

But against whom, or against what, was his soul rebelling if, after all, it wasn't able to protect the thing that he most cherished, that he held dearest? There was no answer. He walked, trying to find himself again, to retrieve those most normal of human feelings, which that same morning had seemed to him so steadfast, so natural and vital. Where did they all go? How could he let them be trampled all over and taken away? How could he let himself be so cruelly humiliated?

The late-in-coming wind from the garden guiltily pushed at his back, sweeping ahead of him and enveloping him in the lilac aroma, summoning longing for his aggrieved love, and reminding him that, with this bitter feeling of loss, he would have to live on.

ALTYNAI

Translated by Lois Kapila

Once we turned onto the deserted street, nothing could hold us back from arguing. He threw his school bag onto the scorched ground, clapped his hands aggressively and shouted scornfully, "Now we know who your girlfriend is!"

I'd been waiting for this. I'd even had an inkling that something like it was going to happen today after school got out. We had exchanged glances far too often in class today, Altynai and I. We hadn't been able to look away and had stared and stared at each other, until classes were over. We might have thought that we had been doing it secretly, that our sighs had been furtive, hidden from those around us, but they were nonetheless noticeable to those who were interested.

And now there was finally proof that all the stories about us which, as we'd suspected, had been making the rounds in class for a long time, were indeed true and were no longer just rumours. Uzumgul could feel pleased with herself now... unless she had nothing to do with it. But who apart from her, Altynai's best friend, could have let the others in on our intimate secrets?

***

Altynai and I usually stole glances at each other at school so subtly that nobody ever noticed. Today, though, our secret must have been clear but we couldn't have acted any differently; after all, ahead of us, like eternity itself, lay our summer holidays and we really didn't want to be apart. Everyone else felt happy summer had arrived, but Altynai and I felt both happy and sad. In front of us lay long months, no, weeks, no – what am I saying? – long, long days of separation.

Matish was already rolling up his shirt sleeves. He always did that when he was getting ready to fight.

"It's just so obvious you fancy her!" Matish, nimble and scrawny but always spoiling for a fight, screwed up his face and stepped firmly forward, ready to pounce at me. "Everyone knows!"

"Don't lie!" I shouted back. "How could ... everyone know? There's no way everyone knows. And maybe it's only you that knows about it, and you decided to tell the whole world, because you're jealous!"

As I braced myself to fend off his attack, I tried quickly to make up my mind: should I fight him today or not? I needed to buy just a little time to summon up the courage for a fistfight at the very beginning of the summer holidays. They were only just starting, and how many more such fights lay ahead? Only Allah knew. This bully Matish and I lived on the same street, after all, and he was known for liking a scrap. If he'd already started to tease me about Altynai, then I couldn't see anything getting better. I was going to end up brawling with him the whole summer.

I rolled up my sleeves too, but for dramatic effect and not because I really cared about ripping my shirt. That didn't matter to me. But Matish had to look after his clothes whatever the weather, because his mum was strict about it. We would both get in trouble for the fight in any case, but if his shirt was torn we would really be in for it. His mum would never let that pass. So, normally, he fought without a shirt on, sometimes even without trousers.

Meanwhile, Matish was already getting down to it. I could see he was seriously in the mood for a scrap. There was nowhere to run; whether I wanted it or not, we were going to have to fight.

It was impossible to predict who would come out on top in our fistfights. Who would thrash who was uncertain, but the consequences were always grim. He was the one picking the fight and he would be the first to fess up. He would tell his mother everything that had happened. And what about me? If I were to go home and tell them I'd been in a fight because of a girl? It would be shameful and disgraceful to admit to already eyeing up a girl in primary school. My Father would box my ears so hard that I would soon get over all that love stuff. I knew my Father. He would say, of course, that it was because of too much spare time. What else could it have been? And then, instead of just once a day, I would have to spend the whole holidays scavenging for fodder twice every day, and bringing back as much grass as our stubborn old donkey could carry.

Of course, the last thing I wanted was to get a punishment like that right at the beginning of the summer, while others would be savouring the endless freedom of the longest school holidays of the year. But you have to stand up for your love, which meant it was unlikely I could avoid a scrap. I decided not to hold my tongue any longer: "You're known up and down the street as a little liar! All you do is lie!"

"I'm the liar?" Matish hollered, in the hope that the whole world would hear him, or at the very least, the whole street. And this quarrelsome, combative little hawk began to take dabs at me.

"Hey, at least take off your shirt! Don't want your mum to know we scrapped!"

But he already couldn't hear me. He breathed into my face with hatred. I still secretly wouldn't have minded avoiding a fight, although his dry, cracked lips, twisted with rage, didn't hold out any special hope for a ceasefire, and I could already clearly see red veins in his bulging eyes. Meanwhile, his well-known-to-me fists popped up, right in front of my unfortunate nose, which suffered equally often from Matish's punches as it did from colds.

Fistfights were normal to us. We would fight in any weather. We always had enough reasons. There were plenty, and if there weren't, then we'd just fight for the sake of it. Why do you need a reason, if you can make do without one?

Life on a single street had condemned us to hang out as friends and to quarrel in the way only neighbours do. When you spend long, summer days roaming a small town, where there are four streets in all, then it is as hard to avoid fights as friendship. Everything is there for all to see. So you have to answer to your mates for every step you take. But Altynai and I had managed so far to keep our love a secret, ever since first class. And now we'd finished fifth year. Matish was right. I'd fancied her from the very first day I'd seen her. But I wasn't about to admit it.

"Who told you I fancy her?" I hollered in response. "She's just a chick. Why would I care about her? Not worth the bother."

"Well, everybody's saying it. And even if they don't say it, I know anyway. You're such a dumbass!"

I knew that now there was no way out of a fight. I clenched my fists.

"Just you say that again!"

"What?"

"What you just said!"

"You fancy her!"

"No, not that!"

"What else did I say?"

"You know, exactly what!"

"I know everything. It's you that's blind, can't see that all the other kids have been laughing at you for ages! You're a disgrace to our street!"

"No. It's you that's the disgrace to our street. You're the dumbass!"

Surprisingly, I was the one to throw myself at him fist-first. Man, I really got it for that from Aunt Mahri. It made it look like I was the aggressor.

We pounded each other for ages, then we rolled around on the ground, and before long we had turned into one dusty tangle. Then we got up again and carried on fighting. At that point Matish, as if tired of the meaningless tussle, threw out the rule book and booted me right in the stomach. Stars danced in my eyes and I couldn't say a word at first. When I did start to speak, I didn't know my own voice:

"What the ... you moron! Wh-hy did you boot me like that, have you completely lost your mind?"

"Sorry," he said, frightened. "It wasn't on purpose!"

I straightened up and whacked him. Matish didn't respond to the blow and, without saying a word, I headed home. It was pointless to carry on fighting.

He stayed quiet a while, and then started to run after me.

"I promise, I didn't mean to, it was an accident, a complete accident! You know I can't control my feet. You're not going to tell our mates about this, right?"

"We'll have to see how you behave ... " I muttered, warning him. "We left primary school a whole year ago and you, like ... like an idiot, are still kicking in fights!"

"But it's your own fault. Why don't you just admit you fancy her? Why're you running around after a bird? Are you not a real man, or what?"

"Just go to hell!"

"Really, you're starting again? You want another fight?"

"Come on then!"

At that moment, a cyclist appeared at the end of the street and we had to call it quits. Otherwise, we both might have got it in the neck for fighting in broad daylight. The grown-ups had been keeping an eye on us, to make sure we didn't fight.

"Let's head to the canal!" I suggested. "We can sort it out there."

We washed the blood from our lips and bathed in the canal water, trying hard not to touch our swollen noses and, once we had cooled down a bit and agreed not to fight any more, we sat down to discuss all the things we would do during the holidays.

"Promise nobody at home will find out about our fight."

"Nobody will find out," Matish answered immediately, "as long as you don't tell..."

Altynai, who had lately occupied an ever bigger place in my heart, would have to withdraw from the scene for the summer, to make room for our boyish games. In any case, I wouldn't see her before September. The long holidays were starting and, for these summer months, she might go away to the country, or stay home and sew, and so to try to see her was just impossible.

She lived on another street, where everything was a luscious green. I always liked to wander down the narrow path past their garden, especially when the tree branches were dripping with fruit. Each season in the garden brought its own delight: in May, tender and fragrant apricots; in June, purple plums, sour but still tasty. July meant peaches, which melted in the mouth like ice cream, while August was everything all at once: grapes, and figs, and pomegranates.

You shouldn't eat too many plums, even if you're offered them; they're so sour it hurts. After a few, you'll be making a silly face. But figs and pomegranates – now, you can scoff as many as you want of them. I, for example, could eat bunches of them. But most importantly, Altynai had for a long time been treating me in secret to all these delicacies. We had moved to the village recently, just four years earlier, so there was nothing yet growing in our little plot apart from some clover and, at night, we had to chase away herds of wild donkeys, which had a habit of trampling all over the little garden as if they'd lost their minds. Over at Altynai's, it was completely different: everything grew in their garden, baskets and baskets full. And I was the chosen, lucky guy who knew the taste of those wonders. As we'd get closer to her house on the way back from school, Altynai would tear off ahead to run the remaining distance, and gain a few precious minutes, so that she would get to the garden first to pick something tasty just for me. She would present these fruits to me, thrusting her little hands through the wooden fence. She had to stand up on tiptoes, stretching as far as she could, even though the fence wasn't that high.

The first time she gave me fruit was when we were still studying in class one. She carried a fistful of plums to me in her own hands. At that time, I was walking along the path by their leafy garden, trying not to look around, and acting like the path was just like any other to me, and that I'd come down it like everybody else, simply because it was the quickest way to school. Quick, that was all. I knew I shouldn't go past every day. I needed to keep my secret. After all, daily strolls could attract suspicion: why is this boy always going along our path when there are so many other roads? But I couldn't stop myself and so I kept to that same path, simply because it was Altynai's.

I would walk along it, weaving through the neighbours' plots, seemingly indifferent, but constantly searching for her with my eyes, desperate not to miss that precious moment when my little darling would suddenly appear in the shady thicket of fruit trees. Once, I glanced over for a second and my heart froze. Altynai, who had run ahead to her courtyard, for some reason hadn't come to meet me. But I could see her. She was standing at the window, cuddling up to her grandmother, and pointing towards me. I felt embarrassed, like I was on show. But Altynai's grandmother looked at me with her wise, old eyes and gave a smile, toothless but nonetheless so pretty that I would remember it forever. I remember it was a stifling, hot day. Midday. Still. Even the shadows were taking cover under the trees. From Altynai's garden alone came a cool breeze. And she ... she was showing me to her grandmother. And the wrinkled face of the old woman lit up, and Altynai also smiled at me, flashing her luminous, white teeth.

The next day, I was scared to go to school. I was afraid I'd see Altynai with her large, tender eyes, and be unable to control myself, and say that I dreamed about her every night, and say that I loved her. But that could upset her, because you're not allowed to talk about love out loud, because if you mention it, it will disappear, fly away. I really believed that. This truth had been revealed to me by my cousin, who was seeing a girl named Nadya. And my cousin had learnt this secret of love from somebody who he trusted, or perhaps he had readabout it in some book for grown-ups, and so I believed him without question. My cousin never said, "I love Nadya." Instead, he said, "I am going to marry Nadya".

I also understood that you can't tell others about your love. After all, it could easily reach the ears of Altynai's brother, who was older than me, or even further, to her father, and then, that would be that. I, of course, couldn't imagine what could end all of this, but I knew – and not just from hearsay – what strict morals reigned over our village, where it was impossible to keep anything hidden. Just try to fall in love here with somebody without the elders' approval, and on top of that, ahead of time, while you're still young. That's why I held my tongue for so many years, and carried on enjoying the fruit presented to me in secret by my sweetheart.

The secret of our love stayed secret for a long time and nobody guessed what tender feelings I had for Altynai. At times, as I was drifting off to sleep, I would dream the whole world was a flood, so that – if only once – I could be alongside her in a single boat. After all, if that ever really happened, we could easily find ourselves together – on a boat or a raft, it would make no difference – and then nobody would be able to say we had done it on purpose, that we had holed ourselves up together by design.

So we, her and I, would sail like that together, and sail ... I would protect her, comfort her so that she wouldn't cry, scared of the tall waves. In my dreams, I would imagine this picture in great detail: when she would start to cry, hungry or deathly tired, I would calm her with various heartfelt words. True, it wasn't clear how long this terrifying flood might last, but I would have liked it to last at least several days so that night would descend more than once for us, as we sailed together on that single boat, and Altynai would nestle up to me, as up to her only saviour, to the most significant person in the world.

I didn't even bother to consider what we would eat. I had obviously decided that in such a situation it really wouldn't be necessary to eat. It would be enough that the girl simply looks at me with her grateful eyes, full of tears – then I certainly wouldn't feel at all hungry. And I wouldn't feel tired. I suspected that she wielded some sort of magic, and, at will, could make me do whatever she wanted. Altynai would give me such a look, as she held out a handful of those purple plums I loved too much, that I dutifully ate them one after the other ... It was as if her look hypnotised me. She, I think, had already guessed her special powers.

I used to dream that, in the end, our boat would reach some faraway shore. I wasn't quite sure what to do next, but I was certain somehow it would all turn out well if we could reach some shore, no matter how unfamiliar. Of all my imagined battles with the elements, whether it was with fires, earthquakes or floods, I always came out the victor, the hero, while Altynai, naturally, with the gaze of a princess, thanked me, her devoted knight in shining armour.

One day, when I was already in class three, I was walking along that cherished path, flustered as always by the anticipation of a meeting.

And on that day, Altynai gave me a present. It was the highest reward for all of the sorrows that I had kept in my passionate, little heart. The prize was, actually, not a handful of plums, but her white, little hands, which I touched then for the first time, for a moment. A whole moment! I felt the indescribable, heavenly softness of her little fingers. We were totally alone. She was standing, fluttering her long, long eyelashes, reaching out her hand from the small plum tree, while I, mesmerised by this fleeting fairytale, froze, scared to murmur even a word, scared to move.

"For you," said the girl, as always, quietly.

Her eyes warmed me with a gentle fire. The sensation was indescribable. Nobody had ever looked at me like that, like Altynai. She had the most beautiful eyes in our class, in our school, in the entire world – and the longest eyelashes. I lost the ability to speak, and for a long time I couldn't shake myself out of it. By the time the haze had passed, she had already retreated to the garden, melting into the thick shadows, and I only just managed to whisper after her: "Thank you, Altynai!"

A year slipped by, and we moved up into the fourth class, and then into the fifth. Every day, before lessons started, Altynai used to meet us in the doorway to the class, checking our hands were clean because she was the *sankomissiya*[4]. Shaking all over, I would hold out my palms for the examination, waiting for this permitted contact. But Altynai would give a smile and let me, a cleanie, go past without a word. Every morning I rushed to school, knowing that Altynai would meet me by the door, wearing her white armband with a red cross and a medicine bag by her side.

My affection for her was growing rapidly and I had few doubts now that the feeling was mutual. When Altynai, one beautiful, autumn day, picked the largest pomegranate in her garden and presented it to me, then the last drops of doubt disappeared. Everyone who went past the house each day had clearly seen how that enormous pomegranate had been ripening, filled with scarlet juice. And the next day, many noticed that the dark-red fruit was no longer there. Nobody said anything, only

---

4   In Soviet times, the most responsible, brightest girl in the class would be appointed the sankomissiya. She would inspect her fellow classmates' hands each morning to make sure they were clean and their nails were neatly clipped.

Matish couldn't control himself. "Who got that pomegranate? Who's that lucky guy who got that treat?" he complained noisily. "If I'd got it, I'd scoff it in a second!"

He didn't guess that nobody had yet managed to eat that pomegranate. I was keeping it safe, because I just couldn't summon up the resolve to tackle it, even though I knew just as well as that dumbass that it could be eaten in the blink of an eye. For a long time I hid that cherished fruit in my room behind some books, as if there weren't sweet, juicy seeds squeezed under the thick, crimson skin but precious, pomegranate jewels. I admired them for a long time, and only ate them because I understood that this offering could start to perish. When I dropped into my mouth the last of the seeds, which were already starting to turn bitter, I felt like I'd become engaged to Altynai. From then on, we were united by something otherworldly. I felt like I could discuss whatever I wanted with her. From then on, nothing could tear us apart.

***

I carried the secret of our love in my heart for four years, all through primary school. Not a single living soul, it seemed to me, knew how deeply I loved Altynai. Maybe only Claudia Mikhailovna, our kind teacher, guessed, but there was no way she would have given away our secret. It wouldn't have been hard for her, our class teacher, to guess what was what. Literature teachers, after all, should know how those in love look at each other. Isn't that why she would glance at us with such tenderness, when Altynai and I, after a moment alone, would appear side-by-side? At those moments, a smile would give her away; she would look at us in a special way.

***

Matish was another story. If he knew something about anybody, then you couldn't expect him to keep it secret, it wasn't his style.

Right then it should have been all about hanging out, enjoying the holidays ... but no way. There I stood, completely exposed, with his help, from head to toe in broad daylight at the very beginning of those glorious days. I was frozen, love-struck, with an uneasy feeling of impending disaster. There was little chance Matish would take pity on me, little chance he would keep his mouth shut. He, it seemed, had learnt all about our affairs of the heart, thanks to the fact that he lived close to Altynai's best friend.

"And what about the others?" I cautiously ventured after we had finished washing and sat in the shade of an old, sparse *toranga*. "What are the guys saying?"

Matish again curled his thin lips. "What's there to say? They aren't saying anything, but now that everybody knows about it, it's game over for you! I don't think anyone'll be friends with you now!"

That sounded ominous. But I wasn't about to break down ahead of time. On the contrary, I was ready for battle.

"Well, they can all go swivel! I don't need anybody, not you ..." I stuttered for a second but I couldn't stop myself, and blurted out what were for me the scariest words ever: "Or Altynai."

Inside my head, I quickly repeated three times: Liar! Liar! Liar! I naively relied on the magic of that simple spell, believing it would protect me and absolve me of my reckless speech. But no last minute gibberish could save me. Once I had said Altynai's name aloud, it was as if I had stepped into ice-cold water, even though I still burned. But the words had already escaped from my mouth. I had, in a way, renounced her ... and it was the beginning of the end of my relationship with her.

What's more, my frenzy had left Matish completely bewildered, I could tell from the idiotic look on his face. There was no point in backing off. I continued my attack.

"And I think I'd like to go to *Pioneer*[5] summer camp. They feed you duck every day there. I'll put on five kilograms this summer, then you'll see! Five kilograms, do you get how big that'll make my muscles?"

"Yeah, right. You're not going to put on weight just by eating duck. I went there last year and it was rubbish. You can eat duck for a couple of days, but give it a week and then you'll be sick of it, but they don't give you any mutton, no chance! And you say you don't need Altynai? You're lying! I know you can't live without her!"

"Says you!" I retorted. "I'll go to the country, to my uncle's, where I've got loads of friends of my own. We'll take our slingshots and shoot at sparrows and swim the whole day in the canal."

---

5   The Young Pioneer Organisation was a mass youth group during the Soviet Union, similar to the Scouts.

"You're not allowed to shoot sparrows, they'll take away your slingshot!"

"No, you can there! It's the country, and it's the grown-ups that ask us to do it! Because you have to keep the sparrows off the vineyards, there are gazillions of them there! Gotta fend them off!"

"So, what, you're ready to spend the whole summer in the country? You're not gonna come home at all?"

I was furious. I was burning to get back at them all then and there, to get them good. It hurt that my intimate secret had been exposed so easily, and I could now become a laughing-stock and not just among my classmates. I'd nurtured this secret for so long in my heart, but now – just like that – everyone would know about it. Because of that, love lost something important in my eyes, became somehow mundane.

"No, I'm not coming back. I'll stay in the country the whole summer. It's just great there, way better than here, no contest."

I noticed that my words had hurt Matish, even the shiner around his eye kind of grew lighter with surprise.

"And what about Altynai?"

"Will you just shut about about Altynai? I don't need her!" I shouted, desperately.

He got up and proceeded to shake the dust off his clothes.

"I'll kick a football around with the other kids, and when it gets too hot, we'll go swim in the river. I'm going home."

"Just make sure that your mum doesn't notice anything, or you know what'll come next. My father always has his belt ready. Pull your cap down a bit."

"She won't notice. And you really think you look normal! Get out of here... you better wash your nose again!"

Matish didn't keep his word. His mother found out about the fight and that same evening, she charged over to our house. She screamed through the whole courtyard, said she hadn't given birth to a son just so that he could be clobbered every afternoon, didn't buy him the most expensive shirts so that other kids could rip them up a few days later.

Those shrieks were quite enough for my father to reach for his officer's belt, which always seem to be watching me from the wall, ready to slither down and be wielded in support of justice.

But Auntie Mahri was already on the way home, her squeaky, shrill voice triumphantly letting everybody know what a bad boy was growing up on our street. Of course, she meant me. I was already stood submissively in front of my father's belt in an attempt to get away with as small a punishment as possible, although it was far from easy in a situation like that.

"To the country! Tomorrow, you'll be off to your uncle's in the country, it's no good just loitering here all summer without anything to do!" warned my father, displaying the power of his thick officer's belt on the wall nearby.

***

I tolerated my exile for a few weeks. But after a month, I was bored stiff and I asked to be sent back home. I was hoping that the dust had settled, but no way. I was met with loud jeers, which I guessed were because there were detailed rumours doing the rounds. Several boys shoved pomegranates right in my face: "Go on, take a bite. We can spare it!"

So I had to retreat again, having survived five whole fights within barely three days. Legs and arms, sure, they get bashed about but how my soul hurt! I tried to seek shelter with my cousin, who'd dropped by to visit, but he only burst out laughing in response.

"Well, didn't I tell you that you've gotta keep love secret! You couldn't, so deal with it. You don't live in a real town, at most it's a dreary big village with the morals to match. You violated the secret of love – and now you're answering for it, be a man and you'll come through."

"But what am I supposed to do, if there are a bunch of them? I'm already tired of their bullying."

"I don't know. See, in town, it's a whole other thing. Nadya and I walk around arm-in-arm, and nobody bothers us, but here, in your place," pondered my cousin, offering no help whatsoever in solving my problem, "you got your own morals."

"But I haven't violated them!"

"So what's the difference? You've still gotta answer for it."

There was no way I could agree with my cousin, so I took my complaints to Uzumgul, Altynai's friend who, being unable to keep the secret so carelessly entrusted to her by Altynai, had set me up with this "splendid" life. I found a moment when Uzumgul was sitting alone in the shade of a grape arbour and – trying to voice all my pain in as brief a time as possible – hissed through my teeth.

"What on earth have you done!"

"Are you trying to say it isn't true?" she said snidely, without the least embarrassment.

"So, you have to tell everybody anything that's true, is that it? Even if you start world war three in our village," I snapped, hinting at the years-long war between her mother and her father's alleged lover. But Uzumgul just stuck out her tongue.

"If you're in love, you gotta put up with it."

"You were jealous, that's why you did it!" I sneered.

"Whose fault would that be!" she retorted, no less fittingly.

I had to leave quickly. Somebody was coming out of their house and what was the point in squabbling with her – nothing to gain from that little tattletale. After all, she'd dished the dirt and she was glad about it. The next day I again left for the country, this time for the whole summer.

***

On the first day of day of autumn, when school started, Altynai seemed to regard me with a strange indifference. We didn't exchange a single word the whole day, and the following day was marked by the same silence. When we again began to talk, we had a normal conversation. I knew that Altynai's grandmother had died during the holidays, and – trying to look grown-up and serious – I expressed my condolences.

But she suddenly said, "You know, it was her who prodded me that first time to present you with something from our garden. She said you're a very serious boy who'll be famous when you grow up. I also believe that – you're smart. But there won't be any more fruit."

"I know!" I said, without hesitating. "But it's not my fault, you didn't have to go and share our secret with your friend! Then everyone wouldn't have found out about it."

Altynai's eyes welled up with tears.

"How was I supposed to know that it would all turn out like this?"

"Well, yeah, I was forced to spend the entire summer away from our village."

"I know," she replied, sadly, "and I missed you. Especially after we buried grandma. She wanted to tell you something but there wasn't time."

The bell rang and we had to go our separate ways. After that, she and I only talked about books, teachers, and other nonsense. But no matter what she and I chatted about, from that day on, a feeling lingered between us that we'd left something unsaid, a silent grievance which deepened over time. It tormented me.

And so my school years flew past, splintered into days, weeks and months. Altynai remained to me the most beautiful girl and, by the time she was sixteen, her delicate, white face had become even more elegant. But then, gradually, she transformed in my eyes into the most unremarkable young woman. I no longer considered her an incomparable beauty and saw her as a friend. The lone thing that still made her stand out from her peers was the enduring sadness in her large, unusually expressive eyes. A sadness that I almost forgot.

My school leaving certificate, with which I left home, was followed by a degree from a university in the capital, and I settled there. But while I was a student I would still go back for holidays and so, from time to time, I would meet my childhood sweetheart. By that time, our sparsely populated village was growing fast and had become a noisy and dusty little town, as they'd started to drill for gas nearby. Our classmates had long ago started their families, while the girls had found husbands and married.

"When are you finally going to get married?" I used to ask Altynai on the rare occasions that we met, knowing full well that she was now the only unwed girl from our year. "Don't forget to invite me to the wedding!" I would joke, completely unaware of the pain I was causing her with my words.

I was amused to recall many of the things that I associated with her, especially the dream of the worldwide flood, summoned only so that I could end up in the same boat as her. Once, during one of my regular trips home, my legs carried me to that familiar garden, and I trod that familiar path, feeling for a moment like a schoolboy. Only instead of a little girl coming to meet me from the garden, there came a grown-up, still unwed Altynai. She smiled, pleased by our unexpected meeting.

"What's this, come for some fruit?" she asked. And, anticipating my standard question about her marriage, as if joking, she added quickly: "I'm not getting married, until you have!"

"Sounds great, me neither," I glibly agreed to her condition. "So, it's a deal."

As she said goodbye, she looked at me sadly. Soon after, I got married and for a long time forgot not just about Altynai but also about my little hometown. I was happy as, for a long time, I'd really only been attracted to city girls. I married one of them after a long courtship, a real, grown-up love. Altynai stayed with her parents for a long time after that. Then, she did the same and got married, but to a guy who was younger than her. They lived, I heard, as the closest of friends. But still, those flecks of sorrow in her eyes reminded me that I had broken the pact we had made the last time we had met. And only after some years had passed did I realise that I couldn't forget her, and then it suddenly struck me – I was, like before, in love. By that time, Altynai already had three children, but she remained as slender as ever.

And when she met me, she would joke, "My youngest loves plums and my eldest, just like you, loves to feast on pomegranate seeds." She didn't guess what a sharp pain that comparison caused me.

Every time I went to that little town, I left with that pain, I carried it in my heart for such a long time – there was no salvation.

THE DEATH OF THE SNAKE CATCHER

Translated by Lois Kapila

On a sultry, summer day in the middle of the silent desert, an old man appeared like a mirage. His silhouette moved slowly, like a shadow, and while there was nothing frightening about him, he gave off an acrid smell of sweat, which disturbed the nose of a magnificent reptile that happened to lie across his path not far away.

The cobra, which was taken by surprise, gave a threatening hiss and was ready to lash out at the old man but, at the last moment, she stopped, and the ritualistic movements of her body slowed. The hard gaze of her little eyes fixed on the man and the more intently the cobra stared, the more convinced she became: this man-silhouette was not so much dangerous, as curious.

Noticing the snake, the old man did something rather strange. He got down onto his knees and, with his hands lifted to his face as if to shield himself from the relentless rays of the sun, which was trying to set alight the scraps of clothing on his body, he began to mutter something unintelligible.

The proximity of the snake didn't seem to worry him in the slightest or his behaviour, in any case, didn't suggest that it did. But the cobra, unlike the man, was wary for her experiences with people had taught her to be vigilant and to believe that in this vast world, which looks so tranquil, there is danger at every step. Her eyes closely followed every movement of the man's body as he made himself more comfortable, still mumbling under his breath. The snake remembered how she had once made an inexcusable misjudgement, and trusted the apparent slowness of a similar, unfamiliar creature that had appeared in the barren desert. That time, she had been caught in his trap and, if the sack hadn't been knotted carelessly... it didn't bear thinking about.

The cobra, squirming, remained where she was, ready to resist any attempt by the two-legged creature to get closer to her. The stranger, though, didn't make a move, as if he already knew how it could end for him. The snake soon got bored of waiting and she had already decided to slither away rather than to tempt fate, when something held her back at the last moment. Perhaps it wasn't the first time she had met this man, who smelt of herbs and wool? Sharp-arched eyebrows blanched from age or the sun, a hooked nose, cracked lips that continued to move almost soundlessly. Yes, there was clearly something very familiar about them all. The cobra softened her supple, wavelike movements, and she began to observe the behaviour of this strange, silent creature even more intently.

And he, leaning his bony, thick-veined hands on the drifting sand, slumped to the ground and began to speak in an unexpectedly melancholy voice:

"I knew it, you know, that I'd meet you. Yes, yes. And I had been waiting for this meeting. I've been wandering the desert, thinking about you and about my fate, and about how every being is born to fulfil the work decided for him from above. A man must manage to fulfil God's will. When you have fulfilled it, you can think about eternity and no longer be scared to die. Death is not the end, after all. It is the continuation of fate, only beyond life, beyond consciousness. That means our fate is not limited by the years we have lived on the earth; to my mind, it can be much longer. The time measured out for us to dwell among the living, continues even after. Some leave life the same moment they breathe their last, and die forever. But some do not, they don't die completely, not everyone. There are those for whom real life begins only on the day of their death. They are either the righteous or the repentant wrongdoers. It seemed to me at one time that the Almighty prefers the latter.

"I appeared on earth some eighty years ago and when they cut the cord a droplet of my infant blood mixed with the earth, with this," the old man brushed his fingers alongside his legs, "desert. It was probably a sign from above, a decree from fate. I had been ordered to live like you, in the unforgiving sands. From birth, both of us, you and I, have been wedded to the sands. And God tied my trade to you all, to you and to the others of your kind. It was forbidden to change anything and, to tell you the truth, I didn't even try. Why would I? My work gave me food and it is, believe me, no worse than others. Although, I really shouldn't talk to you about this, I mean, do you, a speechless animal, even understand the words I'm saying, the words of a snake-catcher. Who am I to you?" The old man sighed heavily and answered himself, "That's right. I am a murderer."

The snake lurched suddenly, as if agitated. But the old man wasn't paying any attention to her. He continued:

"You know, at one time, at the very beginning, I really didn't come to the sands to become a *margir*[6]. I was looking for a miracle. As I went deeper and deeper into the arid desert, I hoped to meet the prophet Kydyr-Ata. I had a desire which I was sure only he could fulfil. So I wandered in the desert for so many years in search of him. Of course, I didn't find a miracle and everywhere I found only heartlessness. I probably grew so wild during those restless years that I came to resemble any number of things, but not a person. Then, people who accidentally stumbled into the sands began to take me for the saint Kydyr-Ata. When they came upon me suddenly in the still desert, people would fall to their knees in front of me, grab me by the hem of my smock, start to implore, to ask me for something, something they needed desperately. At times, it was hard for me to tell them the truth. I didn't have the courage to admit that they'd made a mistake. They were so in need of a miracle. And so, feeling sorry for these people, I was often obliged to comfort them if only with a few words, promises, and then I would say, 'Now go. I will remember your request.'

"People believed so completely that they had encountered a miracle that I didn't even have to dissolve into the air without a trace, as befits a real prophet. These petitioners themselves instantly disappeared from where we'd met, as if they were afraid I would change my mind and take back the happiness and blessings I had just granted them. If, however, they lingered out of curiosity, even when they saw my unremarkable, totally ordinary departure, they took the sight to be something divine, beyond their understanding.

"Did they really believe that I was Kydyr-Ata, the prophet himself? I don't know. And it isn't important. I never tried to persuade them of anything but they, I think sometimes, were not so much desperate for a miracle, as for something to shore up their faith and, having received what they desired, were on top of the world. While I ... I remained here, on this sinful earth, in the endless desert, which was for me both a trustworthy friend and source of nourishment, and an impoverished but dependable place to live. And you, my eternal neighbours and most loyal companions, were always beside me, not that far away.

"But, I swear, I didn't bring you unnecessary suffering, I didn't kill any of you for no reason; if I'd behaved differently, I would sooner or later have

---

6   A margir is a snake-catcher in Turkmen, a man who can tame snakes, draw out their poison and use it to make the healing ointment known as melhem.

ended up cutting off the branch on which I was sitting. For I found myself one on one with the desert, with these shifting sands. To kill is simple enough. The victor, though, is not he who kills his enemies, but he who has learnt to turn them into friends or who walks away refusing to be drawn into conflict. If you are unable to make friends with your sworn enemies, become at least a resemblance of a friend to them. Forgive me, please, for that 'resemblance.'"

As if agreeing with the man, the snake made a movement with her entire body, trying to stretch out fully on the sand, but it was so burning hot at that hour that she quickly recoiled to her earlier pose. The old man, cautiously, with a smooth movement put his right hand behind his back, felt around for his wooden spear, and pulled it closer. The *margir* knew all about the ways of snakes, and he knew also about their weak sense of hearing, and that reptiles are unable to understand human speech but, nevertheless, he carried on talking. He was so desperate to share all that he had inside.

"Believe me, as long as I can remember, I have considered you all to be my closest companions. I can confide in you. I have never been able to become close like this with people." The old man was noticeably saddened by the memories of old grievances. "That's what it's like for me after all: on one side, people, on the other, always you. And, you know, with every passing year that I have lived, fate has pushed me further away from people and closer to you. If there were no you, there would be no me."

The cobra swayed dramatically, her beady eyes intently following the movements of the two-legged creature. The old man tried to wipe the sweat from his face. With all his being, he could feel this dispassionate, cold gaze on him with all of his being. He could feel it, and didn't move an inch. He continued to talk, every now and then lapsing into complete nonsense, his back growing more and more hunched. He was already worn out from both the heat, and from sitting for a long time on the scorched sand. His legs were completely numb. Trying to help out his old body, he carefully stretched out giving the impression he now felt at ease. He then scooped up some of the dry sand in his dry hand, and watched as it streamed through his fingers, like the water that collects in springtime in the pits and takyrs. It was all the man could bring himself to do at such dangerous proximity to a venomous snake.

The cobra understood that in front of her was easy prey, close enough for a quick venomous bite at the very least, but for some reason she hesitated.

The old man's eyes, the colour of flecks of ashes, his protruding forehead, the crimped, lamb's wool telpek on his head, she again and again studied all this with slow deliberation, as if amusing herself and graciously granting a few extra moments of life to this ill-fated victim, but in fact trying to understand, what was going on? Why couldn't she bring herself to attack? How many gazelles and rabbits had she killed in her time? When the occasion arose, her teeth pierced their bodies without delay and without any pity. Once she'd tracked down the prey, it was all done as quick as a flash. The defeated creature would cry out with pain, but for her, a cobra, it was a moment to savour, to inject venom from her fangs into the pliant victim's body. In those instants she would wriggle with enjoyment. Her victim's strength would drain away, it would struggle in agony, relentlessly drawing closer to death, but she would continue to feel a snake-like delight. From time to time, she would manage to reach her victim before it was aware, or understood that death was upon it. And then, when it was already too difficult to save itself from her deathly grip, this ordinary, thin-legged gazelle with a cobra on its neck would dash away as if the earth was on fire under its hooves.

But then the gazelle would gradually start to slow down and suddenly drop like a stone. It would start to convulse. The cobra would listen keenly to the victim's beating heart. She was curious. When would this flutter of flesh become still? It was a triumphant moment for her when, finally – legs helplessly stretched out, and eyes wide open – the creatures would stop twitching and, with their sightless eyes turned in resignation towards the dazzling blue sky of the desert, fall silent forever. Then the cobra would slither away and wait, until hyenas or jackals approached the free feast. She needed them, couldn't get by without their help in her cruel meal. And, of course, they never let the snake down. At the first scent of carrion, they would gather with cowardly howls and immediately throw themselves on the gazelle's body. The cobra would remain hidden, and watch their revolting banquet with disgust – until it was time. As soon as these predators, jostling amongst themselves, ripped open the gazelle's stomach, she would suddenly swing towards the pack and send the dirty, reddish-grey gluttons scattering in all directions. They would whimper as if in pain, but she quickly forgot about them and everything else, eagerly reaching for the gazelle's warm, blood-filled kidneys. Kidneys with blood, what could be tastier than that?

Once satisfied, the snake would look sternly at her "friends," the entire pack pathetically whimpering a little distance away. *I used your claws and teeth, otherwise I wouldn't have been able to get to that treat by myself, but now – have your feast.* With one final, terrifying look of her cold eyes, she would slither away, generously leaving the gazelle's torn-up body to these desert beggars. She wasn't interested in what they would do next, how they would growl with insatiable greed, how they would frantically gnaw at the bones, how they would drag them into different corners, tearing out of each other's mouths bloody scraps of that luxurious gift, which seemed to have come from out of nowhere. Their disgusting habits were so repulsive to her that the snake would hurriedly slither away.

Wolves were different. They never touched her prey. When they saw a gazelle with an enormous snake clinging to its body, they would simply bare their teeth and run away. It sometimes seemed to the cobra that these proud predators felt something resembling compassion towards these tortured animals. Maybe they even despised her for her alliance with the hyenas and jackals, which she used for her own ends, if only to get her favourite treat. Wolves, these angels of death which brought fear to all creatures in the desert, would hunt their own gazelles rather than covet the feasts that any hyena or jackal had found.

Here in the arid sands, each creature has its own rules and habits which, taken together, make up the laws of the desert. Naturally, each has its eternal enemies. Even the marmots. Although they spend almost their entire lives underground, digging out burrows and passages, crawling around, hiding from large, evil predators. Sometimes, though, their underground sanctuaries become their graves; the sands are suddenly shaken under someone's feet – perhaps a horseman, or a camel herder – and collapse, and bury the unfortunate creatures in their own burrows. To venture out of their burrows is also dangerous. But sometimes their blind eyes are irresistibly drawn to the light, to the sun. From time to time, it is as if they start to miss the crimson dawn and the flowers, which appear for a short, dream-like time in spring across the dunes. Then the marmots decide to take a perilous journey, even if it is only to the surface of the earth. But there, a fox has long been lying in wait.

The cobra had seen all this time and again. But she had never interfered in others' business; she had always been a cold-blooded, detached observer. Her eyes looked at the world indifferently, dispassionately. She never felt pity, although she could consider the marmots unfortunate, the hyenas cunning, and the jackals cowardly – traits she knew because she recognized them in herself.

***

The cobra had many enemies, very few of whom would dare to get close to her. But this man had completely overcome any feeling of fear, or was it completely unknown to him – fear? On the hot sand, under the sun hardened in the sky, there they were, like two statues forgotten by time: she and him. Both the storyteller and the listener were tense, keeping their eyes trained on the other. The cobra's full attention was now fixed on this man, literally just a stone's throw away from her. Could her greatest enemy be this very creature, stinking of wool and sweat? How long would he sit there, testing her patience? And why was he still muttering through his dry, cracked lips? Could it really be that he didn't know she had already had enough of him? But why had she stayed there, in front of him? What attracted her to this man? Could it really be only because instinct told her it wasn't her first meeting with him?

And the old man continued:

"I don't wish you had met me earlier, when I was even stronger. It's only natural that my most rebellious snake remained free. I don't regret that I haven't yet managed to catch and tame you. I know nobody is permitted to attain the highest level of perfection in their craft. Sometimes, it's true, it seems like you have understood everything, you can do everything, but time passes and you learn that perfection is as far away as it was at the very beginning of your journey. Sure, it might be painful, but that's the way it is.

"I, for example, never thought that you, the largest and most powerful snake in this desert, would listen patiently to me. If I had raised you myself, fed you from my own hands, then probably, for the first time since this endless desert was created by God, there would have been harmony between bitter enemies. Then two of the strongest living creatures would have been tied, one friend to the other, you and me. Listen to the sound of that word, 'friend'. That's what they say when one creature needs another, and can't get by without him. I regret that since I mastered my craft, although I relied on you, my friends, at the same time, I didn't fully trust you. I believed more in the ancient ways. We have such a tradition, a snake-catcher has to catch, and..."

The old man pursed his lips, thinking, hesitant to say the word "eat", but then continued all the same:

"... eat the largest snake around. Then he will never die from a smaller snake's bite. So the biggest among you sometimes became my dinner and guaranteed my safety."

The cobra undertook some kind of strange manoeuvre, attempting either to slither a little further away from the old man, or to express her displeasure. The old man flinched. He understood that she hadn't liked his words. But he continued his confession:

"They consider you all to be treacherous. And I thought that, too, and lived with that belief my whole life. Maybe that's why I'm still alone in my twilight years. I just can't reconcile myself to the idea that I don't have one valued companion, not a single person who can hear my thoughts. But then you ... are listening to me. Although eighty years living in the world, it seems, should have been enough to get used to earthly loneliness. But I can't, it turns out I still need the company of living creatures, maybe even people. But they have shunned me. My work scares them so much. But why? How is it worse than other work?"

The old man fell quiet and lowered his eyes. His back once more hunched over, bent even more sharply. In his once-mighty hands bulged thick veins, like the exposed roots of a willow on the banks of a canal whose water has taken another course. The old man searched his memory, recalling with distress how people, who had rejected his friendship all his life, still could not get by without him, and would come to ask for his help when they were sick. They shamelessly used him for his rare gift.

The most remarkable incidents remained forever in his mind. He can remember to this day, down to the most trivial detail, how long ago in his younger years, one of the rich beys, a leader in the area, fell seriously ill. And one day, this man, the most influential figure in those parts, sent messengers to visit him, a poor, ostracised, *margir*, snake-catcher. He had been sheltering from the midday sun in his ramshackle hut as was his habit at that hour, when he suddenly heard the powerful voice of a stranger: "Saparli, Saparli-*margir*!"

The man called out insistently:

"Saparli! Come here! Come out into the courtyard!"

Saparli realised that the man calling him was scared to come into the house. So the old man – who actually wasn't yet old at that time – complied. The visitors had only briefly explained the essence of the situation, before they ordered him to sit on a horse that had been saddled especially for him, and ride behind them. The road was long, and the riders drove the horses hard. When they dismounted near the wealthiest house in the area, Saparli guessed who had summoned him. The young snake-catcher saw the master of the luxurious home, his body contorted with pain, and understood that something was seriously wrong. Once they were alone together, he set about examining him, this all-powerful man twisted with severe rheumatism. Then Saparli asked to go home, and they immediately brought another horse. The next day, at first light, the snake-catcher-doctor returned to the sick man with fragrant medicines and snakes, and rumours began to circulate that the snakes were enchanted.

The *margir* quickly began his mysterious ritual, opened the wicker basket and began to whisper something, running his hands over his face and pounding the sides of the basket. From inside, the cobras extended their haughty heads with menacing hisses. Saparli then hurriedly set about casting spells, while rubbing *melhem*[7] into the sick man's skin. The *bey* thrashed about, groaning with pain, and tried unsuccessfully to escape the *margir's* strong hands, which were as adept at tightly gripping people as snakes. Was that not why people ran away if they happened to come across him? The *margir* was crafty and resourceful, just like the snakes in his care. People were scared even to argue with this taciturn young man. Who knows what could happen?

The sick Kerlen-bey also acted like he didn't trust him at all, and thought him a dark, even strange, figure. But once illness had him backed into a corner, nobody was able to help him, and there was no other way to lessen his hellish suffering, he decided to try this last resort and endure this torture.

Saparli attended to him for exactly three months. For exactly three months he treated him with his balms and "enchanted" snakes. And each time the doctor left, the patient fell into semi-consciousness, left without the strength to say a word, to curse his unloved healer. His wife would carefully lift his head and pour an opium brew from a large tea bowl into his mouth. The patient would just lie there, with his eyes shut and moan from time to time. His health, though, gradually improved, and the day came when people witnessed how a once-helpless man, who had been bed-bound the whole year, leapt onto a horse by himself without any help. Everybody was astonished and afraid. Rumours spread from house to house about the peculiar, inscrutable art of the *margir*. Some said that he had cured

---

7   Melhem is an ointment made using snake venom.

the patient with cobra bites, others that he had given him roasted snake to eat, and the ointment that had been rubbed over the patient's body was a complete sham, meant only as a distraction.

As always, the women engaged with particular zeal in this idle chatter. They had a special reason. At some point, Ogulhajar, a close neighbour of the local leader, went with a jar to the well, and told all the women there something very strange.

"I have no idea what Saparli-*margir* did to him, but the unlucky guy isn't interested in her anymore. That's what his old wife told me in secret. She said he's probably running after a younger wife. Unlikely, when the poor man looks like he's in pain, frowning all the time when he's just walking around. So that means it's completely ..."

The women began to tut-tut and fuss, while Ogulhajar gave a nasty smirk.

"Let's thank God that our leader is alive at all. Each to his own, as they say. At the end of the day, you can live without that, probably..."

That was the day it started. Like a wind sweeping through the thickets of rushes on the banks of a canal, the men began to look askance at Saparli with undisguised suspicion and some even began to despise him. Just imagine that: a man does a good deed, cures an unfortunate patient, but what a pitilessly heavy cost.

***

The former patient himself was completely unaware of all the gossip and hostility. He would pleasantly greet Saparli. After all, if it hadn't been for the *margir*'s snakes, he – the leader, Kerlen – would have been rotting in the ground. It may be true that they're repulsive, slippery creatures, possibly connected to evil spirits, but when your whole body is twisted by hellish pain, when not just your hands, but your fingers won't move, you're ready to sell your soul to the devil himself, if only to feel well. Now he, Kerlen, can sit in the saddle as if nothing ever happened, his chest puffed out, and can again delight in the fresh breeze which caresses his face, and listen to the delicate, silvery jangling of women's trinkets, and – most importantly – can take in those dear, sweet nothings of his young wife, Sahragul, when she massages his legs or barely noticeably bites her moist lips, the contours of which show temptingly through her fine, Persian shawl.

Once, a strange thought flickered in his mind: if he threw a Persian shawl over the heads of Saparli-*margir's* snakes, they would probably be as graceful as the most beautiful women. After all, cobras are no less elegant than women. But then he was scared by his inappropriate thoughts. "God forbid," he quickly repented, "How could I think such a thing! And I'm not even sick anymore!"

Kerlen's earlier arrogance had vanished, and once he even drove a dozen sheep himself to the door of Saparli's hut. He was in such a good mood that he would often give expensive presents to his healer, much to the great envy of others. But those who saw this were puzzled. Was Ogulhajar making up stories? You can expect all sorts from these idle women. They have nothing to do, so they gossip away.

Others, considering themselves more insightful, said, "It's not necessarily that the *margir* did something bad to him. Don't they say that if a snake enchants you, then you'll forget both your children and your wives? Nothing will save you. Why does he need wives now? They don't matter to him and he's doing pretty well without them."

Some said that Selim, the village *mullah*, once saw a cobra enchant a lark and the bird just dived head-first into the snake's mouth. Had something similar not happened with Kerlen? True, he said that he's scared of the slippery creatures with their piercing, icy stares and frequently flicked, poisonous tongues, but who will rely on the words of a man who has already called on the help of magic powers?

The leader, though, forced people to treat the *margir* with respect and, if only for a time, forget about their animosity. Saparli was happy, and even started to think about marriage. There was a girl in the village who wasn't scared of his snakes, which endeared her to him. But there was one hitch. Her parents didn't want to hear about such a son-in-law. Even Kerlen-bey couldn't convince the stubborn couple to abandon their deep-rooted prejudices. The snake-catcher was as much of a pariah as ever. People continued to look at Saparli-*margir*, the saviour of their leader, with contemptuous suspicion. They imagined that after long years of association with snakes, he himself had taken on their traits: swift and supple, with noiseless, smooth movements, with eyes that bore through you – it was difficult for a mere mortal to withstand such a look. Hadn't he also learnt how to bite? It wouldn't be surprising, given the company he kept.

And so it continued. Only those who were facing an agonizing death without these arcane medicines went to him for help, while the rest avoided him. People obstinately refused to acknowledge his rare expertise, careful not even to touch his ointments, although they often needed them.

***

And now, many years later, sitting in front of an enormous snake, the *aksakal*[8] mused, "How many years have passed since I learnt my trade? Was it a mistake to choose this path? And what is true now? Is it as it was or as it was remembered? In any case, who can answer these questions? Nobody. These events were long ago carried away by the sands. Yes, and many witnesses to those days when they shunned me have already departed this earth. But I am here, living, and sometimes I think that I don't need anything now – not honour and respect, not praise, not my talent for healing, nothing. I want to live, simply live, regardless of everything. Although… did my life have meaning?"

The old man's lips curled up into a quivering smile. In the cobra's round, cold eyes, drops had begun to grow, as she enigmatically swayed in front of him. The next minute, sensing the movement of the human hand, she momentarily swung to the side, then drew herself out straight again when the old man took his cap off and put it down beside himself on the sand. His lips began to move weakly again and he spoke in a whisper.

"I'm looking for meaning? Well, look here, I'm sitting and talking to you, and you are listening, and that is meaning."

The cobra calmed down.

The old man felt that his strength lately had noticeably faded and a strange peace had been penetrating deeper into his body, his muscles were heavy with weariness, and they only grudgingly obeyed him. He would hole himself up in his ramshackle hut for days on end, and then he would come out, staggering from weakness, and wander around his home, weakly lifting his legs. It seemed that the main purpose of his present life was to be a recluse. In summer, he hid from the sun, in winter, from the cold, and always, from people. For some time, he hadn't wanted to see anybody at all and could go without food for days. When it was time, he ate quickly out of habit, rather than desire, swallowing down anything that accidentally came his way, even if it was completely tasteless. It was the process of eating, more than hunger, which reminded him he was alive. As he chewed the hardened

---

8 An elder.

chunks of roast mutton he had stored away for winter out of habit, he ever more frequently caught himself thinking it was the last time he would open the jar, the last time he would spoon out the stew, the last time he would gulp it down. *In the future, I guess, there'll be no need.*

And nobody special had brought him any sheep for a long time. The leader, Kerlen, had passed away several years earlier. It was boring now without his ardent protector. People had eventually lost interest in him. It was like he had been buried alive, his notorious reputation condemning him to loneliness. Solitude had killed him long before real old age. But for as long as they haven't buried you, haven't put you in the ground, it is as if you are still alive, and you won't get away from that. You have to prepare food, make the fire, but to do that you need to collect saxaul wood, and so you force yourself to live, as if unwillingly, but through these movements you are drawn into life and make peace with it and with its laws.

Not long ago, it's true, he had felt a real, sharp onset of hunger and trembled, his hands and legs fell limp. With his eyes closed, he lay unmoving on the earth for almost a whole day and night and didn't notice he was lost in a lingering, exhausting dream. But once he awoke, he felt brighter, like something had happened to his body while he had been unconscious. A dull ache of hunger in his stomach forced him to look around with his eyes, to find something edible. His eyes travelled searchingly, anxiously over the bare walls of his dwelling, over the dirt floor, until they reached a coiled, meaty snake.

That evening, he was close to desperation, on the brink of compromising his integrity: in the frying pan, lumps of mutton fat were already spluttering. The snake-catcher pulled himself together at the last minute, although the snake clutched in his hands had already almost departed from life.

"No," he said. "It would be better to die of hunger than to betray my craft. My calling is to cure patients with snake venom, not to take snakes' lives. After all, God did not give me the gift of friendship with them to waste them as food!"

For many years, snakes had been his best friends, with whom he had shared both his sorrows and meagre joys. They had lived fearlessly in his home, from time to time, showing off like young newly-weds in front of their *margir*-master, from whom emanated secret, magic powers that tamed them. And he, Saparli, like a man tired of life, didn't want to see them anymore, didn't want them in his home. He trapped them all, one by one, and with a heavy sack, set out into the desert. And there, far from the village, unexpectedly for the whole tangle, he gave them back their freedom. The old man watched with a heavy heart as the snakes slowly slithered away. One of the beautiful creatures didn't want to stay in the desert, and followed behind him like a loyal dog. The *margir* had to chase her away, again and again.

The snake-catcher could see her eyes the whole walk back. The old man came to his senses only once he reached the door of his deserted home, in which there was no longer a single living soul. He felt a profound sense of melancholy. He spent the time from dawn until sunset completely lost and didn't know what to do. In this life, he no longer had anybody or anything, only his sad memories of the past.

He spent several days in this state. And then, the desert called to him. The yellow, shifting dunes, alive in his imagination, whispered to him. He heard their tender, hoarse voices, but couldn't make out their words. It was pointless to resist. He got up and looked around, deciding to clean his home before he left, possibly, forever.

"It's not good to leave your home untidy. A visitor might suddenly stop by and peek in," he sadly joked aloud.

Out of habit he placed several flatbreads and a clay jug with water in a sack, and left on his journey. He held once again in his hands a wooden spear, the only weapon that he took out into the desert.

＊＊＊

The village had hardly disappeared from sight when the old man's heart began to pound with its earlier, agitated rhythm. He began to hurry, like a man on his way to see his young wife. He had never had a wife, but now he could clearly understand what it meant to feel sick in anticipation of a long-awaited meeting. From *barkhan* to *barkhan*, from dune to dune, his path lay in the depths of the vast sands, where human feet had not yet trodden. He went further into the desert. The well-beaten road had soon been left far behind.

Finally, the old man let himself catch a breath and take a little refreshment, a flatbread moistened in water. The only tracks across the visible expanse were those of the native residents of the desert. *The desert doesn't remember anyone for long. It wipes away the tracks of everyone who walks here, not burdening its memory with anything, he thought. How many people have passed through these sands? Yet you won't find their tracks here. Is it not the same in life? A man dies and nothing remains after him? In any case, of Saparli-margir, there won't be any traces on this earthly sphere, of that he is almost certain.*

He tried to chase away these unhappy thoughts and remember how, for weeks, at times without sleep or food, he had pursued some large snake or other. Before she gave in to him, she managed with diabolic ingenuity to get away, to dodge, to creep, to bury herself in ravines, to burrow into the sand. It wasn't easy with them, the giant snakes, either at the moment they were caught, or when it came time to milk them, to draw out their venom. But his spear never let him down, and his hands were as strong as his eyes were sharp. And then, once deprived of venom, the snake in an instant became docile, like a bride who has just entered her groom's house. She could still threaten, hiss, get angry, but all this was only a pale reflection of a former life, a longing for a freedom gone forever.

***

The cobra swayed and pulled herself up to almost her full height, ready to jerk back sharply and attack the old man from the side, when she suddenly noticed a wandering steppe spider, creeping towards the old man from behind. The cobra momentarily froze. Pale from tension, the *aksakal* attentively, fixedly continued to follow the snake's movements, clearly unaware of this impending attack by another unforeseen enemy. The cobra lifted its head, as if signalling the danger to the man, but he didn't move. Then she puffed up her hood and swayed forcefully. But the old man didn't think to look away. He didn't take his eyes off her, off the cobra.

The steppe spider was already very close. The cobra should have immediately, without delay, gone for the old man, in order to force him to jump up and so save himself from this vile enemy but, in a strange trance, she froze. She remembered how the jackals and hyenas had thrown themselves onto the gazelles she had killed. Now she herself was the one to watch and wait, calmly hanging back, while someone committed murder.

A moment passed and the old man jumped up, arching his weak body like a young man. His hands reached towards his right shoulder blade, where the steppe spider must have stung. The cobra, in any case, sprang backwards, although she understood – now she had nobody to fear.

"Widowed snake!" the old man gave a strangled cry, one moment crouching down, the next jumping up again. Then he collapsed onto the sand and writhed. "Widowed steppe spider! Widowed scorpion!" He repeated an old curse, which people in those parts would use if they didn't know what had bitten them. "Widowed scorpion, steppe spider... black widow..." he continued, incoherently whispering, trying to protect himself from the worst, finally guessing what had bitten him.

The old man seemed to be trying to understand something inexplicable – it wasn't his snake, after all, that committed this terrible act. She couldn't do it, no, not her... The old man suddenly sat down, a flicker of resignation in his expression. Soon, his eyes darkened and he stared at the cobra. Could they see or not? There was no way for the snake to know, but she was still afraid of the snake-catcher, as if he could throw himself at her as easily as before, take away her freedom, draw out her protective venom. The *margir* still exuded a potent authority, and it was hard for the snake to free herself from this magic. When the man finally crumbled to the ground and fell silent, the snake waited still longer. Soon the large steppe spider crawled out from the hem of his white, calico shirt. Deftly scurrying over the shifting sands, it quickly disappeared into the shadow of a nearby saxaul tree.

And only then did the cobra crawl up to the man. His face was calm, and the little corners of his mouth were marked with spots of white saliva. Beside his body lay a canvas sack, which gave off a familiar smell. Now she understood. That was it, that smell that had both riveted her to the spot and stopped her from attacking the man. It made her head spin, muddled her imagination and, it seemed, possessed the same terrifying power as the eyes of the *margir*. The snake crawled around the sack, inspected it from all sides, even tried to stick her head into it but, frightened, immediately recoiled. She understood that you don't escape a second time from a trap like that. She, after all, had already found herself in that sack many years earlier, but then she had simply been incredibly lucky. He had only tied it loosely ...

The cobra again stared at the lifeless body of this worn-out, two-legged creature but still chose to draw further away from him, for she trusted only herself and the strength of her own venom. It still wasn't quite clear whether he was dead or not. What if he had just fallen silent for a short time so as to catch her and shove her again into this unforgettable sack?

The cobra remained a while longer, watching over the body, until she was bored with the stillness of the man and slowly, in circles, began to move away from him. And soon, she had completely disappeared into the eternal silence of the sands.

LOVE STORY

Translated by Youssef Azemoun

In a little village next to the forest on a mountain's foothills, there once lived a mother and her child. Her husband had fallen from a cliff while chasing a mountain deer, so the bereaved woman devoted all her attention to the boy, on whom she doted night and day. When he cried, she pressed him to her bosom, and if he fell as he skipped and played, she rushed to gather him up in her arms, asking:

"Oh, my little one! Have you hurt yourself anywhere?"

The mother had a strong feeling that she would overcome her difficulties and happy days would return to her home. With such overwhelming hope, how could she not succeed in protecting her son against any dangers that might loom over him?

The mother made every effort to bring up her child without making him feel the loss of his father leaving him hungry and miserable. To earn her living she served the well-to-do people in their houses – she wove rugs and carpets for some of them and took up cleaning in other houses. She also designed and made felts when she needed to save as much money as she could. Although she was working very hard to make her wishes come true, she did not get tired, nor was she oppressed by how difficult a job might be.

The boy lived up to his mother's expectations, he was tough and brave. He was growing up fast. Caught up in hard work, the mother did not even notice her son come of age, until one day she saw he was suddenly a young man and that in a couple of years his moustache would grow! The mother was somewhat relieved when she saw her son grab the best silk kerchiefs in jumping contests, and receive the highest prizes for wrestling at weddings. She heaved a sigh of relief, saying: "May the hard days be a thing of the past!" Then, with the money she had earned with the sweat of her brow, she bought her son a steed whose beauty was unrivalled in the village. She placed a *kinjal* with a white handle at the waist of her son, who rode his steed wearing silk clothes, and was becoming a well-known figure around the village.

"Take this, my son, it is a keepsake from your father! The blade is from the steel of Merv, the handle is ivory and the silver is from Urgench. If you use it for a good cause, it is said that it will do you no harm. Your late father cut out the heart of a deer with it and brought it to me to eat while it was still beating."

How could the girls not stare at this attractive young man wearing a hand-made red robe with a sash around his waist and a pair of elegant, traditional trousers, and riding a steed? When the mother saw the village girls biting their sleeves and sighing as they looked at her son passing by, her heart would beat swiftly with happiness.

The young man, though, showed no interest in any of the girls. He sensed the breeze on the tips of the horse's ears, and delighted in the peace of the countryside and the speed of his horse. He enjoyed hunting in the valleys, traversing the mountain paths like a falcon. The beauty of his village, which lay in a crease in the landscape where the countryside met the high mountains, was a source of overwhelming joy to him; he could not even imagine that any other joy could exist.

Then the outlook of the young man on the thoroughbred gradually widened, and he began to notice the beauty of the neighbouring villages too. And in one of these villages, one day in the late afternoon, near a mountain spring, he came across a beautiful girl, the like of whom he had never seen. It was love at first sight – it happened as soon as they noticed each other. Those who saw them meeting alone thought them a comely pair, a pretty girl and a good-looking young man: God, what an elegant couple! They might have been made for each other!

Travelling frequently to meet the girl he had chosen, the young man turned the road to the neighbouring village into a pilgrim's way. When the lovers were well-known in the villages, the mother, who was living on the threshold of different, happy days, listened to the sweet beating of her heart and waited for the days when her son and the girl would agree to unite their fates. She took pride in this situation: now she would send a message to the parents of the girl, the two families would become extended families and after that they would hold the greatest wedding ceremony ever! Of course, everything was ready for the wedding. Then she would tie her foot to the cradle and rock her grand-children for the remainder of her life...

However, for some reason their bond of love did not mature. The girl loved the boy, but was in no rush to marry him. Whenever the boy asked the reason for this, she would always say: "If I knew you loved me sincerely,

I would marry you" and leave him in suspense. Finally, one day in the late afternoon, they met at the usual place, and the young man stood before the girl and asked:

"Why this uncertainty? How long are you going to make me suffer? When will you say what you think?"

The girl shot him a deep glance:

"I have one condition, if you fulfil that, we will see..."

"Tell me your condition, I will definitely fulfil it, but do not hurt me more than this!"

The beautiful voice of the girl came out extremely hoarse:

"No, you cannot fulfil it... The condition I am making is too difficult for any human being to fulfil..."

The young man earnestly entreated:

"Tell me. Someone else might not be able to do it, but I will! If I cannot do it, spit in my face and say 'Shame on you!' "

The girl fixed her attractive eyes on the young man's eyes:

"My love is different from other people's. For this reason, it will be matchless."

"What kind of a condition is that?"

"The condition is different, you know..."

"Tell me, let me hear it! Around here, there is no one who could push me into the dust in a horse race, make me fall while wrestling and beat me at sharp-shooting. So who else apart from me could fulfil your condition?"

"You know I can do all that too, you know that well..."

"Then, tell me your condition!"

She began: "If I say..." then held back a little before continuing. "No one in the world should have any right over you other than me! No one would or could love you more than me, even your mother who gave birth to you. However, you always attach more importance to your mother than me, you never stop talking about her!"

The young man was knocked senseless. He was confused and could not find any answer to what he had heard. Because it was a fact that he loved his mother; he did not even attempt to conceal this. So although he said, "No, I do not prefer her to you!" his response was also hesitant. "She is my mother and you are my beloved. You occupy a special place in my heart, there is room for both of you!"

The girl frowned, clouding her brow that was like the wings of a swallow:

"No, that is a lie! There cannot be room for two women in a man's heart! You have to choose: either me or your mother! I do not want a husband who is his mother's baby! If you really love me, stand by your promise and prove that you really love me. If you cannot do this, you will have yourself to blame …".

The young man interrupted anxiously:

"True! True! True! But how can I convince you? Would you believe me if I tore open my chest and put my heart in your hand?"

The beautiful voice of the girl echoed him:

"No, let your heart stay in your chest!"

The young man, who could not grasp what the girl was saying, asked a second time, more forcefully:

"What do you need then?"

"Just look at this man in love! Do you still not understand what I'm saying?"

"No I don't, keep talking, I want to hear!"

"If you want to hear…," the girl hesitated. "If you want to hear… If you really love me, go and bring me the heart of your mother!"

In the twinkling of an eye the young man, whose hand had reached for the handle of his dagger, sighed deeply and gave a groan that shook the mountains. The sound made the colour of the moon fade; it oppressed the mountain rocks, making them hunch their shoulders.

Cursing the girl and the terrible condition she had set, the young man returned to his village, his head lowered. He did not eat for a few days, did not come out of the house and shrank into his bed. His mother watched with distress as her son grew paler and paler, and shared his pain. But how could she help her son, who burned with agony in the fire of love?

After a few days, the young man realised that lying in bed would not alleviate his suffering, and so once again took the mountain path to the neighbouring village. He confronted the girl and begged her:

"Change your condition! I will do whatever you want me to do!"

The girl stood firm. After that, the poor lover kept travelling the distance that separated him from his beloved: there and back, there and back… One evening, he went to the girl and knelt before her:

"Have mercy, set a condition that I could fulfil! Ask me to chop off my finger, I would chop off the one you showed me! Ask me to cut off my arm, I would do that! But do not meet my love with cruelty – unheard-of cruelty!"

The girl's response was firm:

"No! Be a man, keep your word, you said to me earlier: 'If only you would tell me'. I put my condition to you, what are you talking about? When my desire comes true, I am yours, before that I don't exist. You should know that no woman other than me in the world could have anything to do with you! You would be only mine! Why should I share you with someone? Go and bring your mother's heart. I don't care about anything else. If you cannot cope with my condition, you should blame yourself!"

The young man once again went back home. The girl shouted after him, as he moved away, his head hung low:

"Bring it when it is beating! Otherwise I won't accept it..."

Knowing that he would never be able to fulfil this condition, the young man decided to throw himself off a cliff. He whipped his horse on towards the precipice. Then, remembering that his mother's tears would flow like a flood, he held his horse back. He took to the mountains, and lived in the mountains and the countryside. Then he returned home and slept, no longer eating or drinking. He languished day and night, lost his appetite and could not sleep, distancing himself from the joy of life. He gave up on the world, and turned away from it. Yet his suffering did not go away, his love for the girl did not diminish, on the contrary, it grew stronger. He sent a message to the girl that he would not be able to live without her: wait for me at the usual place at midnight, this evening...

Although she could not take away the pain of her son, who suffered the agonies of love, the mother suffered with him. She worried about her son, looked anxiously at his pale face, ate her meal without much appetite and, hoping for better the following day, settled quietly in her bed.

The mother, overwhelmed with fatigue after the day's hard work, slept as soon as her head hit the pillow. Although worried about her young son, the tired mother slept deeply. Even a heavy storm in the middle of the night did not disturb her. Despite the heavy lightning and thunder, she slept peacefully and felt safe with the knowledge that her son was nearby. And so, when the *kinjal* with the white handle pierced her chest to the hilt, the mother could neither scream nor shout. When her son removed her heart and began to walk away from her, she could only stretch out her arm after him...

The young man had no time to waste, he had to give his mother's heart to his beloved while it was still beating. Nor did he have time to take a look at the body of his mother left behind. He jumped on the horse, which was waiting at the door with the bit between its teeth. He travelled on, following the mountain paths through the dark of night. The hooves of the horse resounded in time with the thunder, rousing the valleys buried in darkness and the cliffs with their heads hidden in the obscurity. As he galloped with his secret, his sole confidant was the storm, which shook the trees, rolled the rocks, dug the earth and sifted the world. He was in a great hurry, kicking his horse to run faster: go, go, go!

His horse seemed to understand everything and ran like a mad thing, carrying this young man, who held in his hand the heaviest of gifts as a token of love. The moon in the sky showed itself occasionally, trying to throw glances of light onto the mountain cliffs before hiding behind the clouds.

Half of the dark path was behind him… And then the speeding horse tripped over a tree root, which had been left bare by the rain, and rolled over. The young man fell from the horse and was thrown among the rocks. His mother's heart, released from his hand, flew through the air like a shot bird, and fell down to the path…

The young man jumped up in panic, ran over and picked up the heart. The heart was not beating. Believing all his efforts had been in vain, he moaned with fear. But the mother's heart had not died… When the thunder stopped and the surroundings fell suddenly quiet, the warm heart began to beat once again in the palm of the son's hand. Then a weak voice came from the bleeding heart:

"Oh, my little one… Have you hurt yourself anywhere?"

ONE OF THE SEVEN IS A SCOUNDREL

Translated by Youssef Azemoun

Mingled with the sweet tunes of the songbirds, time pours down from the sky as a pleasant sound. Aware of the approaching heat and the peace of the early morning, the birds of the steppe trill with delight. The larks sing sweetly over the cornfield till weary, and descend in search of food.

The sweltering summer heat seemed intolerable to the men lying on the horse cart moving along the dried mud takyr path, some holding their coats and some their sheepskin hats under their elbows. Jummi, the harvesters' team leader, warned the sleepy cart driver holding the reins:

"Come on, keep driving, Tashli, don't sit dozing and try to get the passengers to their destination before they're scorched!" he chided. "You'll drive alright when the midday sun digs into the tops of our heads. What's the matter with you? You wouldn't care if the whole world were flooded. Try to be like other people!"

"Choov, you miserable animal," cried the cart driver, grabbing his whip. "You suffer all the trouble and I get the blame! Come on, move, or I'll hand the reins to Durdy Egri – then you'll move!"

The harvesters laughed. Durdy Egri disliked this remark.

"All you do is moan and whine at people," he protested. "You don't know anything else."

"There must be a reason for my complaint," Tashli retorted. "If you don't want to hear any moaning, you have to keep your word!"

The harvesters could not understand what the argument between Tashli and Durdy Egri was about. Durdy Egri was unreliable – you could not hear a word from him that was both honest and correct. That was why in the village he was called Durdy Egri – Durdy the Crooked. This nickname had in a way turned into his surname. Tashli's peevishness towards him was not good... Jummi the team-leader tried to quell the disagreement. Spreading his old coat, he sat in a more comfortable posititition.

"Listen, Tashli," he interceded. "Moaning is not what matters. What matters is our reaching the village as soon as possible. Think of the time since we left the village. Separation tires children too. They must be anxiously waiting for us."

"Mothers of children too," volunteered Ojar from where he was lying. "Those poor creatures must be staring at the road to Tejen!"

The harvesters seemed to have woken up and movement on the cart looked lively.

"Hey, if you're serving this government," said Tashli, turning back, "what's the rush for? This government does not build a dome over your grave. If they find a pretext they send people to Siberia one after another."

Ojar nudged Hakly sitting next to him and dismissed what Tashli had said:

"You think you've found someone to build a dome over your grave?" he exclaimed. "Come on! This government is still destroying the domes already built. And you expect something useful from it. You should be happy if the government does not pull your house down on top of you."

"Hush," the team leader interrupted him. "Tashli and Ojar, mind what you are saying! See what is happening around you. What we have been hearing is appalling. You know some people from the other village were arrested and sent to Siberia. May God protect us from even worse! We hear of arrests everywhere. I feel lucky about the lack of informers among us. One informer can ruin our lives. Still, be careful. As they say, 'walls have ears and ewers have eyes!'"

"There is the collapsed castle and there is the black ewer!" cried Ojar, interrupting the team leader and pointing to the ruins of a castle in the distance. "When you find an informer you can find both the wall and the ewer."

Jummi the team leader remembered the saying "One of the seven is a scoundrel" and anxiously looked around and tried to calm things down.

"What can I say? These days one of your two eyes can become your enemy; it is better to keep quiet. Suppose I didn't say anything and you didn't hear anything. I'm truly rueful, black bird mine," he quipped.

"There, the black figure has appeared," Ojar interrupted him, pointing eastwards. "Look there comes a wagon," he added.

The people on the cart thought this was a joke and they were looking at Ojar rather than in the direction he indicated. Jummi the team leader straightened up.

"Ojar, will you never grow up?" he said sulkily. "When will we see you as a sensible adult?"

"Open your eyes wider and you will see. Don't look at me, look at the road!" declared Ojar, extending his hand eastwards. "Over there, do you see that wagon? It looks as if they are coming from Tejen..."

Seeing the strange cart, Jummi the team leader moaned and tried to quell the distress that had overwhelmed him.

"I wish we could have taken another road to Tejen..." he said. Then he spoke in a tone to encourage himself and the people near him:

"So what? Let it come if it is coming! Haven't you seen a wagon before? It may be from Tejen or Merv – what difference does it make? After all, they're all carts! If it comes, it will pass by. These carts are always seen on this road. In the distant past, there were times when four carts could meet at the same intersection. What's so strange about it?"

No one answered Jummi the team leader's question. People began staring at the wagon coming from a distance and everyone tried hard to find out what kind of cart it was and what kind of people it was carrying. The slanted eyes of tall, thin Hakly were focused at that moment on the harvesters. As if not believing his eyes, pursing his lips, he took another look at the people on the cart. No more nor less, they were exactly seven people. This worried him even more than before. Perhaps he studied their faces carefully because he felt as if he was seeing his co-workers for the first time. He too panicked: "One of the seven is a scoundrel, one of the seven..."

Being a person with keen sight, Ojar described his impression of the people on the cart, which was approaching by a short cut:

"It's not a cart it's a wagon. There are soldiers with weapons on it. The glint that we see must be from the barrels of their weapons..."

"You and your ideas," Jummi the team leader scolded him. "I hope it's not an NKVD wagon. Ah, Tashli, you didn't speed up the cart when we told you to. I told you so many times not to sit there dozing off. Now let's see you whip harder! If we stop specially and let them pass, God knows what they will think. It's better if you try to cross the intersection before them. We can do it – we're ahead of them. Whip it harder!"

"Choov! With seven of you on the cart, do you think it will move any faster? Choov, may your fodder be nothing but bran!"

Jummi the team leader looked at the cart driver angrily and began to rebuke him harshly:

"We know who those words should be used against, but alas, now is not the time. Move, don't act the fool!"

The whip began to whack the horse's flanks but failed to make it move faster – it continued as slowly as before. When the harvesters saw the tarpaulin-covered wagon, with pale-faced people swinging their legs on it, begin to come closer, they began to fear the worst. Because they had no doubt that what had appeared in their midst in the middle of nowhere was the NKVD wagon which collected "enemies of the people". This scared the wits out of the harvesters. The whip in Tashli's hand lost more of its bite. The harvesters' cart crossed the Tejen-Ashgabat intersection in front of the NKVD wagon. After leaving the main track behind, they all heaved a sigh of relief, as if they had rehearsed it before. Tashli felt a new strength in his hands, and in order to leave the intersection sooner and lengthen the distance between the cart and the wagon, he lashed the horse twice. Put under pressure, the horse began to drop its dung as it stumbled on. This attracted the attention of the people on the other wagon.

Either from the heightened panic somewhere on the cart or decrying the driver's belated zeal, Jummi the team leader looked askance in Tashli's direction. The harvesters' main task now was to avoid meeting the glance of any of those seated on the approaching cart which was already near at hand. The NKVD wagon suddenly turned towards them on the winding path, so that the prisoners seated on it could be seen from the back of the cart. But no one had the slightest wish to look at the "passengers" on the wagon more than necessary or God forbid you might meet the glance of someone you knew. What then? What a pain to attract the gaze of those poor wretches you cannot do anything to help! Everyone wanted to leave behind this section of the journey, to get away and forget those who had fallen into the clutches of the people catchers. The harvesters were relying on the speed of the horse harnessed to the cart. As if sensing the people's panic, it made incredible efforts not to let them down and tore ahead. But the sun's heat would not let it keep up the speed and soon its withers and flanks were covered in large drops of sweat showing that its strength was not limitless.

The officer on the other wagon, as if trying to remember something, focused his attention on the harvesters, who were moving away. He ordered the driver of the two-horse wagon to stop. The soldier immediately pulled the horses' heads back. He jumped down, placed the reins on the shaft and shouted at the harvesters:

"Stoyat! Ostanovityes! Stop! Pull up!"

He raised his hand and began walking straight towards the harvesters, his boots creaking unpleasantly. He stopped in front of them, took hold of the gun on his shoulder, and began asking questions in broken Turkmen:

"Why you move so fast? Why you running away? Who is fugitive on the cart?"

Tashli, who panicked when he saw the soldier staring at him, did not know how to answer. He was tongue-tied and gulped as he tried to suppress his emotions; he swallowed his spittle. The soldier began to look fixedly at the panic-stricken harvesters one by one. They were seated in front of him, their sun-burned faces looking as if they had turned into cast iron. He behaved like a man in the bazaar trying to buy a horse; his looks were suspicious and thorny. This made the harvesters panic further; they all kept quiet. Jummi the team leader, remembering that he was responsible for the actions of those sitting there, finally managed to overcome his anxiety and answered in a language similar to the soldier's – a mixture of Turkmen and Russian:

"We not running away, kemendir, we been reaping. Too much rabota and the children waiting for us in the village. They need bread kushay. Being so excited about returning home, we may have driven rather fast. Now we stop stoyat, kemendir."

The blue-eyed young man in military uniform smiled:

"I am not the commander. The commander is coming. He will talk to you. Ne dvigatsa, don't move!"

"Alright, alright," Jummi the team leader stuttered. "There is nowhere for us to escape to, kemendir. When you said stoyat we didn't even move."

Then the officer strode over and before he reached the cart Jummi the team leader greeted him with:

"Idrasti, kak dila kemendir, how are things?"

The NKVD officer, his eyes blue as the sky, smiled insinuatingly and shook his head slightly:

"Zdrasti, dila kak sazha bela, things are white as soot."

At this point Jummi the team leader admonished Tashli:

"Ah, Tashli, you've ruined my life as it is! Did you get a look at their eyes? They haven't come here for nothing. How many times did I tell you not to sit dozing off sniffing the horse's bum?"

At the team leader's gripes, the cart suddenly jolted forward. The harvesters, as if they had just awakened, looked at each other with some fear. The officer did not like this state of affairs. The young soldier took hold of the reins.

"No going! Where do you think you are going?"

"We are not going anywhere," said Jummi, immediately trying to pacify the situation. "We will stay here until you say go. The horse may have shied."

"Our man wants water. Vodu davay!"

The harvesters all reached for their jugs. The team leader, who had caught a glimpse of hope, said:

"Oh, if water is what you want, no problem!"

The officer and the soldier gave each other a meaningful look and drank water from the harvesters' jugs. Then the officer asked the harvesters sitting there:

"Who's the boss?"

"I'm the boss, kemendir! Pomogay! Let me help you!" said Jummi, half rising.

The officer made a gesture meaning "follow me" and turned round his red-starred pentagonal military hat. Apparently obeying the order, Jummi the team leader followed him. At some distance from the cart they stood facing each other. The officer immediately put his request to him:

"Znachit tak… We are going to take ten enemies of the people to Ashgabat. Over there, on the way, one of them escaped while urinating. I am now taking nine people. One more is needed."

At this point he put one hand on Jummi's shoulder, and the harvester felt he had become shorter.

"You bring a man and give him to us, so we have ten people. Here's the document, the telegram saying we must take ten people from Tejen to Ashgabat You must find one person from the people on your cart."

"It is not possible, kemendir!" replied Jummi, perplexed. "Would there ever be an enemy of the people among the harvesters? These are honest, law-abiding people trying very hard to survive on hard labour. They have no idea about being enemies."

The officer took a look at the cart and pointed at Tashli:

"Come on, you give him to me!"

"No, it can't be!" exclaimed Jummi in broken Russian. "He is a poor man, they have eight malenki children, his wife is bolnoy, ill in bed."

The officer was obstinate. This time he pointed at Durdy Egri.

"Then you give him to me!"

"You mean Durdy Egri? No, it is not possible, kemendir. How can you separate him from his home? His son got married last year and he is suffering from tuberculosis. Jummi the team leader made a great effort to cough. "He is not in good enough shape to be an enemy of the people. He has many children."

"Why you no have an enemy of the people? They can be found in every village but you don't have one! This is podozritelno, suspicious! I will go and see the boss. You don't have any children, yes? I will take you! If you cannot find one enemy of the people among these seven, then you become an enemy of the people! You are an enemy!"

On the sun-tanned face of the blond officer with leather boots and khaki uniform signs of cheerful acquiescence noticeably diminished. When Jummi the team leader noticed this, his legs began to have difficulty holding his body up and he was tongue-tied. The blue eyes of the officer, like the blue sky, seemed to have turned into a whirlpool in a deep sea ready to devour everything. The team leader looked at his harvesters with a sad expression on his face and tried hard to fathom the fear that suddenly loomed over them. The lives of those on the cart were surely the heart of the matter. Whenever the officer pointed at them, they began to tremble, because they noticed that the soldier immediately approached the one whom the finger was pointed at. The longer this situation continued, the more they lost their patience over the unbearable misfortune that might threaten one of them. Everyone curled up, remembering his home and family, and longed to return home to be among his children. But obviously, one of the harvesters would not enjoy such a situation. Then Durdy Egri suddenly jumped down from the cart, to the harvesters' surprise. Durdy Egri went up to the soldier:

"Kemendir, ya pomogay, let me help you!"

The soldier looked at Dury Egri with some suspicion as if to say "what kind of a person is this?" But then he made Durdy Egri follow him and took him to the officer. When he went up to the officer he whispered something in his ear. Then the NKVD officer, leaving Jummi the team leader in an anxious state, pulled Durdy Egri aside while the soldier returned, whistling, to his previous position. The men's anxiety increased. They could not understand what was happening, and sat hunched up. A terrifying silence prevailed on the cart. After listening to Durdy Egri, the officer pointed at the harvesters. The soldier came up to Hakly and put his finger on him and the officer shook his head. Then the soldier's finger was pushed into the chest of Ojar and the officer once again shook his head. The officer pointed to the man in charge of the horse, and when the soldier indicated Tashli the officer nodded. At that moment the bayonet of the soldier's gun was pushed against Tashli's body...

"Get off the horse! You are going with us!"

Tashli was in a state of shock when he heard these words. The harvesters noticed that his face had turned pale. He gave a sad look to those on the cart, but who could help him in any way? The harvesters tried not to look at Tashli's face, they looked down and lowered their eyes and, sitting in the cart, they began to scratch the wooden parts of the cart. After that, constantly looking back, Tashli walked ahead of the soldier. He was taken to the wagon with the tarpaulin cover and pushed into it.

The officer took Durdy Egri to the same place. The harvesters watched him have his fingerprints taken on a piece of paper. It was not clear why the officer did not wish to send him back after that. The harvesters thought they were trying to fix a place for him among the prisoners. The men's anxiety grew. Feeling sorry for the horse, covered in gadflies, they waited for the incident to reach its conclusion. Finally, Durdy Egri returned. The harvesters cast an eye over him with some fear. They pulled sour faces as they felt some unusual movements in their bodies. Durdy Egri's somewhat wide face had turned into the face of a dead body. Although the distance was not so great, he looked as if he had gone alive to the NKVD wagon and returned dead. There seemed to be no life in his face. Moreover, he seemed to be ashamed of being among those people. He took the whip and mounted the horse.

"Move, you good for nothing animal," he cried.

The horse cart moved slowly with a squeaky jolt. Soon the NKVD wagon took off too and began moving towards its own destination. They followed with their eyes, with some trepidation, the wagon that was taking one of their friends to a place of no return. They were thankful they had survived this grievous distress. Durdy Egri began to whip the innocent horse, as if it to blame forthing.

"What kind of a nag are you? Come on, choov!"

From within himself he now called on God for help, and trembled. He was only concerned with avoiding the responsibility for the damage he had caused. If anyone asked him about it he had the answer. He would say "I saved you". However, troubled by the pangs of his conscience, he tried to overcome his anxiety by constantly whipping the poor horse.

"Come on, you stupid animal, Eugh! Eugh!"

Durdy Egri did not know how to reconcile his human conscience with the deed he had just committed, and tried to calm himself down. "What have I done wrong? Nothing. I have only done my duty. The will of the authorities is the will of God. For it says in the Koran: 'All authority is of God.' So it is all quite simple, and there is no need for me to worry about what will happen in the next world."

God was merciful, He would forgive him. But what was that sepulchral silence? What was it for? Could those pitiable creatures do nothing but keep silent? But the longer it continued, the more oppressive the silence became, only showing that people's silence is not the most innocuous of all possible penalties for an offence. And at length he could only explode:

"What, have we lost our tongues? Why are we so silent? I saved your lives, so thank me!"

But they were in no hurry to thank him, and he still had no suspicion of the meaning of this dogged silence surrounding him. He did not realize that his relationship with them would henceforth shift to a new plane and would never be the same as before. And looking back at the wagon being swallowed up in the dust of the road, he considered he had made an easy escape from the danger hanging over them, himself included:

"I have saved myself and also eluded the need to repay an intolerable debt. Can that be bad? As for the others – what do I care for them, so long as they don't try and squeal? He who has the authorities behind him has no need to worry! Now the only thing left to do is to sweeten God up. But that is probably feasible. It's not the first time God's forgiven people. If it comes to that I will offer Him another loaf, perhaps even two... I'm generous, and God loves the generous. Then we'll see who he finds nicer in the next world! With God it's much simpler. It's worse if you're in debt to people..."

He continued talking to himself to the creaking of the cart.

"If he had not demanded the repayment of the money," he thought, "Tashli would be a nice person and could have carried on living. I have only myself to blame for what happened."

He recalled how last year, when he gave his son in marriage, he borrowed some money from Tashli. No-one else helped him apart from Tashli, who lent him the money. For a moment doubt flashed in his mind:

"Perhaps I behaved badly, perhaps I should not have done that?" He was not sure he had acted properly. In a fit of pique he vented his anger on the dumb animal, lashing at her with his whip.

"Move, you old nag!" he hollered. The mare broke into a gallop, as if a veritable demon had mounted her. The harvesters looked around in alarm, as if they did not recognize their native steppe. They looked helpless in the face of the harsh adversity which had suddenly landed on them.

"No, the mare will not endure such a gallop," murmured team-leader Jummi. "She must be well nigh exhausted..."

Meanwhile, perched on the mare like a bird of prey, Durdy Egri drove her as fast as he could, as if trying to break free of the murky silence pressing upon him.

"Come on, you stupid animal," he roared, coughing and casting a contemptuous glance over his shoulder at the harvesters. "That's how you drive the horse! Eugh, Eugh!"

Team leader Jummi repeated to himself the same words: "No, the creature will not stand that for long. An animal is not a person, to endure everything. We will hardly be able to finish the journey, we're doomed to be stuck half-way. We're doomed..."

RYAZAN HORSERADISH
AND TULA GINGERBREAD

Translated by Richard Govett

Black thunderclouds had rolled over the town and the rain had started spotting. The bazaar folk were flustered: the Russians took shelter, the Azerbaijanis lit up cigarettes, the Vietnamese opened Chinese umbrellas over their numerous little heads, and everyone started jabbering.

"Oh hell..." Baba Toma swore, glancing at the sky as she continued walking through the solid ranks of market traders in search of food for herself and her husband.

"Rain again! I'll get drenched through and catch my death of cold. You can't cadge an umbrella off anyone. And the prices! These traders will get their own way eventually – they'll starve us to death..."

She knew what society needed now: no matter who, but someone who was at least on your side and thought like you, otherwise she would be unhappy and on her own.

But there were not many here to talk to heart-to-heart. She sometimes managed to engage someone in conversation, pour out her heart, gabble about life, as she liked to put it, but people could not stand close contact with her for long, and soon "peeled off" from her. That was another of her expressions.

There were few locals at the market, they were all some sort of interlopers – only the customers or assistant criers were of her own kind. But Baba Toma was not too disgruntled about the lack of people to talk to. People are all much the same and there were quite a few with whom you could just strike up a conversation about the daily grind. This was now the same for almost everyone, so even complete strangers would suddenly get talking, complaining to each other about the hard times and everything that was going on everywhere.

But of an evening she and her disabled husband were left all on their own, and then life would turn into non-stop misery – crabbed and tedious.

"Killing them would be too nice!" Baba Toma would say, sitting on her half-collapsed sofa. Thus would she deliver her grim verdict on the politicians who would almost every evening broadcast on TV what they were now doing with the country and what they were planning to do with it in the future…

Her husband took all these goings-on excruciatingly. Groaning and fidgeting in his wheelchair, he would raise his crutch above his head, threatening those appearing on TV with divine retribution one moment and rough justice from a sinister Stalinist troika the next.

"You need Stalin! he'd get you crawling! Raving hotchpotch!" he would exclaim, trying out the old stentorian voice he came back from the front with ages ago.

At such moments his eyes would blaze militantly, even aggressively, but his voice was not as triumphant as it used to be. He had long ago ruined it with drink and could not roar but just break into a nasty rumble or often just wheeze:

"Sons of bitches! look what they're up to, what they've done to the country! they're ruining it, they've torn it to pieces!"

To which Baba Toma would answer cogently:

"If you were them you'd do no better, maybe even worse. After all, I know you."

"You know me, bloody Baba! Tula jamka muffins is all you know about. And don't hog the TV!"

"Stop your boar-like behaviour or you'll go without supper!" Baba Toma would tease him with her Tula expressions.

"I'm tired of feeding you. If you went to the bazaar yourself you'd realise what a curse it is finding food for two. It's a free for all. Those blasted Vietnamese guzzle and don't leave a crumb for anyone else. The Azerbaijanis are the same – they won't leave anything. Our Russians are better, they never eat everything up. They always leave something. You just rummage and take it. The day before yesterday one left a whole pizza and me and Duska had a feast!"

"So why didn't you bring some home for me?"

"We scoffed it on the spot. Do you think we're not human and don't get hungry? All critters have to eat, not just you, remember! Just because you ruined yourself before time, eh? Otherwise your back would be OK and your legs would work. When other chaps were ground down by life they picked themselves up, but you just collapsed and wouldn't get up. Otherwise we could have both gone on the parade as we used to on the 9th May – an honour for you and me. But now everyone's forgotten us."

"You, Baba, should chatter less and pick up your broom and start cleaning again so we can eat properly. And tell Duska I can't work but she could for a bit. Better than begging with outstretched hand."

"If I don't stretch out my hand – you will stretch out your legs and die! I'd gladly work but who'd take us back now the market's in charge? Nowadays the youngsters sweep with their skirt hems. At least many people remember me and Duska as workers and respect the memory of us. That's the only reason you haven't perished of hunger yet. And don't give me all that talk!"

"Don't go on at me! I'm not dead yet and I want to live to see those scoundrels eat manure or their own pooh."

"You'll never live to see it. Anyway, what about those Caucasians and Vietnamese..."

"The country hasn't been ruined by Caucasians and Vietnamese!" her husband interrupted her, straining the words through his teeth.

"It's our lot, the Russians!"

"Nowadays not all Russians are our lot," his wife retorted with a frown. "There are some who won't even talk to us. Remember a couple of days ago I almost broke my back dragging home a full bag?"

"Course I remember, how could I forget when we had enough to eat for several days?" her husband replied. "You don't forget suchlike in a hurry."

"Well, it was one of ours, a Russian, gave it me. He threw it right at my feet. He didn't like me asking for money!"

"That sort should hang," the husband wheezed again without taking his eyes from the TV.

"What? then we'd only have the likes of you and me and Duska left and the country would be taken over by the Vietnamese and Caucasians."

"You don't understand. I tell you, it's not the Vietnamese who put us on the slippery slope, or the Caucasians. They haven't got the teeth for the Russians."

"Who is it if it's neither of them?"

"Let's have some nosh and I'll tell you." The husband rolled his clumsy wheelchair to the dinner table. The wheelchair pitched to one side or the other according to which way he leaned, and all the way its weight made the old floorboards creak pitiably.

Baba Toma gave a sly smile.

"Wouldya' like some caviar and sweeties?"

Baba Toma had from childhood loved a miscellany of sweets, and was not indifferent to them in old age. Yelena, the local confectioner, knew this and Baba Toma had sometimes managed to purchase or wheedle a few sweets from her. From the very first day she had teased her husband with them. The first night they got to bed after a noisy postwar wedding, the bridegroom ordered her in a commanding voice to undress, and without thinking she blurted out:

"But wouldn't you like some sweeties?"

"What, sweeties at midnight?" said the bridegroom, not understanding, and roughly seized her by the behind.

"Here are my sweeties and nice Tula gingerbread! I'll treat myself to them every night – just you try and stop me!"

Toma, who had barely come of age, could not blink an eye before he threw her on the bed and possessed her by force. Then he asked:

"You've had your sweeties! Satisfied now?"

Like a beaten bitch she whimpered in the dark for an hour or so and asked shyly:

"Where did you learn that?"

But the young husband was already in a deep drunken slumber. Half a century had passed since then but never again did she ask that naive question which she posed the first night out of sheer feminine stupidity. The *muzhik* could learn anything anywhere – he'd come from the war! And where there's war there's plenty of improper knowledge.

Then, waking up next morning after the wedding, she was too timid to complain to her young husband about his roughness. Then she let it go and there were countless other instances. But the rudeness she endured on her first night was eventually remembered with actual nostalgia: it was like coming into the big wide world...

Her husband always had a peremptory tone and straight after the wedding she had to get used to it. At that time he was the most eminent bachelor in the village – decorated and a hero all on his own account. All the girls were fascinated by him, literally sighing at sight of him. But after just a fortnight of being fancy-free he made his own choice. One summer evening, waiting till the gang of girls were returning from the *kolkhoz* field, he went onto the road and loudly announced:

"I'm going to marry you shortly, my lovely! So tell your Mother! But don't treat me as a farmhand; I'm marrying you, not the farm. We're Ryazan folk, we're thick as thieves!"

He didn't even wait for an answer but turned and went off, medals jingling on the broad chest of his army shirt.

"Oh, Tomachka, you've made it!" her friends chirped. "Wow! in a flash! And what a lad, gleaming with medals like an archangel!"

Toma was in seventh heaven – she really had hit the jackpot. No wonder many envied her having found real feminine happiness. Her husband's roughness she took for masculine strength and privately decided she would be ashamed to complain.

In the first week of life together Toma had to throw herself completely on the victor's mercy. This is how it happened:

"On all fours!" her husband commanded on the second or third night.

"What's that – all fours?" the wife did not understand. "Am I your mare or something?"

"On all fours, I said!" the husband repeated decisively. "Chop-chop! orders are orders."

"But wouldn't you like some sweeties?" she let slip without thinking of the consequence.

"You'll get your sweeties now!" the husband exclaimed, forcing her to her knees and elbowing her in the back painfully.

Toma resisted, but a sharp blow to her bottom made her howl and collapse. It was like being hit in the arse with the butt of a "Kalasha". That was how she remembered the heavy hand of her victor all her life. That night she submitted to her husband and capitulated, holding out the white flag. For a long time.

Much water had flowed since then and so much had happened that the whole past now seemed unreal. It also seemed unreal that they were childless. They had been unlucky. It turned out that as a young girl in the war she had had a cold on the kidneys. Miscarriages occurred when there was not far to go and whenever she got pregnant she would miscarry again. She tried everything to carry the baby to full term: she saw doctors, frequented white witches in villages, but to no avail, and she had to accept her fate. Once or twice Toma brought up the subject of adoption, but her husband was adamant:

"Since God isn't giving us His own, why feed someone else's? Anyway, I'm happy with you, my foal-less little mare!"

But he soon forgot he'd said he was happy without children. Tedium and world-weariness set in, he drank shamelessly, got into brawls, womanized and stayed away from home. In short, he became a notorious daredevil. At first Toma was ashamed of him; after all, they lived in a village where everyone knew each other. But then everything rapidly changed with the encroachment of the town, and by the beginning of the 1960s it had swallowed up their village. Toma felt more comfortable – there were far more drunkards and philanderers like him in the town.

***

Her husband went on swearing at the TV:

"These sons of bitches know nowt about statesmanship."

"So you know more than anyone?" she butted in "Who do you think you are – Lenin and Stalin put together?"

"I'm telling you, they don't know nix about politics. We had a battalion command..."

"How much longer do we have to hear about your battalion commander? You trot him out year after year! And I don't want to hear about your generals – I've had enough! They were likely turfed out of high office and lost their posts. I can see them now sat in wheelchairs bellowing at their wives, while Vietnamese and Caucasians are in command in the bazaars! That's what you're like, you kamanbats. The country's migrated to the bazaar and you and your kamanbats to your wheelchairs!"

"You always were thick," the man insisted pig-headedly. "However long we've been in the town, you're still all village and your wit hasn't grown by one gramme. How many times do I have to tell you it's not the Vietnamese but the Chai-neeeze" – he stretched out the word while pulling his eyelids like slits with his fingers. "They're only pretending to be Vietnamese! The Chinese can also swindle by pretending to be Russians."

"With those eyes of theirs?" mocked Baba Toma. "Don't invent fairy tales, kamanbat!"

The man was put off his stroke a bit but a burning desire to continue the argument would not let him retreat.

"Don't try dipping into politics! It's not women's business," he fumed indignantly. "You wait till they demand the Far East from us," he continued significantly, changing to a whisper. "There likely are no

Vietnamese here at all. The Americans got rid of them with their famine terminator, no, what d'ya call them... toxic chemicals!"

"No use scaring me with the Chinese, let your kamanbats get headaches about that. But I have to think about you, wretch, and get food every day. If I thought about one thing after another you'd starve on me."

Having exchanged their usual "courtesies", they went to bed. Come the morning, Baba Toma, as if going to work, made her way to the market – where else was there to go for food?

Arriving at the bazaar, Baba Toma usually walked along the rows without thinking. She went wherever her feet took her, she did not mind where she went. She did not realise she had trailed all the way to the end of the longest row of stalls and was still empty-handed. She walked for ages in vain. An empty day. Would she and her husband have to go to bed hungry again? And this damned rain! when would it end? And where had Duska disappeared to? She hadn't died, had she? God forbid! In the past few days she had been a bit poorly, looked really peaky and walked oddly, sort of sideways, not inclined to speak and just drawling something under her "potato" nose. This appellation belongs not to her but Baba Toma's husband who hails from Ryazan country and compares everything, good or bad, to something familiar from his neck of the woods. Force of habit. In retaliation for "potato-nose" Duska nicknamed him "Ryazan horseradish".

Baba Toma was offended at first, fair enough, but later actually got used to it. She would be happy to tease him with "Buzz off, Ryazan horseradish!" And he would retort with: "Are they dried up, those Tula muffins and nibbly gingerbreads? No fear! they're still soft and biteable and if you dunk them they're really good!" That's how he would indulge her and Duska's ears whenever he wanted to curry favour and earn a quarter bottle of vodka. "A quarterless *muzhik* is like a baba without lipstick," he would say, enjoying his own inventiveness when the threesome were gathered round the dinner table. And on rare festive days they had a great time when the "gingerbreads" were dressed up and powdered and "horseradish" had shaved and put on Eau de Cologne. At table "kamanbat" would shower compliments on his "gingerbreads", saying no women in the world were more beautiful than Tula women and none at all could cook better than they. The "gingerbreads" were always glad of this praise and would chuckle aimiably and say "any fool can cook a fowl".

Baba Toma went on wandering round the market without trawling anything but a couple of stuffed pancakes, and no-one had proffered her any money today. She had to eat the pancakes herself – she needed the strength to go round the market. But eventually, wet through and tired out from trudging round the thinning rows of stalls, she headed for home.

On this wet autumn evening she walked unsteadily like some sort of drunk, of which there were quite a few round here. Waiting for her at home was a surly, hungry husband. But there was nowhere else to go, so she trudged the usual way back to the dilapidated wooden house built with logs by her grandfather long before World War I. Toma was in fact born in it during the years of Collectivisation and later brought her spouse to live there. Despite her son-in-law's cantankerousness, mother-in-law loved him and forgave him his numerous transgressions. She liked him being practical. Despite his farmhand jokes during courtship he got to work on the house even before the wedding: he renewed the lintels while keeping their old Tula patterns; he renovated the plinth, replaced the rotten floorboards, and changed the thatch for an iron roof. He even built a small bath-house in the courtyard. Mama could not be more pleased with her son-in-law and quipped: "When a *muzhik* asks, he reaps and mows grass." But dear mother-in-law did not live with them for long. She soon fell ill and died, to their great sorrow. So Toma remained with her husband in the family home, and had passed her whole life within its walls. Now it would seem that she, too, would be carried out feet first like her parents before her.

All the way home she was wondering how to pacify her husband when he got in a rage on seeing his wife return empty-handed. It is so hard to feed a hungry husband with words. But their destitution might be over. Why, the President had promised to increase pensions, and he was a man of his word. He had actually promised to lie on the railway line if the people were any worse off. It is said that his assistants only just managed to dissuade him. Well, thank God for that, or there'd be hell to pay. Why should we pay for him lying on the rails? We had enough to pay for that woman – what was her name... oh my God, Anna Tolstaya was it?

"No, lady, not Tolstaya – Karenina!" she was awoken from sleepwalking by a passing lad in a cheap Chinese padded jacket.

"Get off!" she swore heatedly. "D'you want to give me a heart attack, damn you?" Only then did she realise that she had been moaning aloud all the way and she thought it was just privately.

"Did I ask you?" she inquired even more angrily. "I know who I'm talking about and that's good enough for me. So you fold your wings back into your Chinkie jacket and be on your way and me on mine."

The young man was already gone without trace but she was still muttering.

"She showed us up to the whole world, the flirt! Hey! give her a bit more loving! Wouldya' like some sweeties? But the President wants to lie on the rails too! You feel like saying go on, lie on them. He's a good *muzhik* though, eminent, and speaks plainly like us. Now he's promised to throw the people some more cash. So from next month my Chapayev and me will get a raise and then we may have enough to eat – well, to live like a human being for half the month. It'll be easier then. Enough for cigarettes, why not? No baccy for soldier boy like shaman with no rattle toy... For vodka perhaps, or maybe better not or he'll be commanding when he drinks, just like kamanbat! And I should drink less, you can't drown your sorrows and things don't work right, your legs hardly walk and neighbours are still more standoffish. The bazaar's a godsend, you might even have a field day with them treating you to food or drink. They also give money although sometimes they call you a beggar like that lad who threw a whole bag of shopping at my feet. What a pity – I touched his sleeve, I didn't mean to. But did I stink perhaps?"

Tomorrow she would go to the market earlier. She would wear her best dress and tie on her black shawl – let them think she has some kind of sorrow, then they'll take more pity. But she would have a good sleep so as to get there first thing while people are still in the money. Then someone might give those dollars. But today I'll build up my strength with rusks and hot water, I'll make do with what there is. There aren't a lot of rusks but a couple each should be enough. But Duska has vanished somewhere. It's boring without her and she's a bosom pal. I'll go and see her in the morning.

Her husband met her right at the doorstep, in a turmoil, with a tense expression, gesticulating wildly in his wheelchair, waving his crutch, urging her to hurry.

"We've got a visitor," he declared, letting Baba into the house. "You'll never guess who!"

"No need to guess, it'll be Duska. She's always at it, as soon as I'm out the door she's sneaked in here. She's so annoying, she's left me on my own and gone missing. You work better in pairs and now I'm back with nowt," she exclaimed, chucking her empty rag bag at her husband.

"Why are you in such a rage, chatterbox? You always were a fool," her husband said in his usual wheeze, wheeling his way towards the bedroom.

"This way, quick! You can see with your own eyes how your Duska feels! She turned up here complaining she was poorly and then, without any warning, she died right here! How could she, is that the way friends behave?"

Baba Toma sighed wearily and asked:

"But why did she lie on our bed?"

"She asked to. I could hardly pick a fight with her, could I?"

"Well, leave her be. Nobody will give her a funeral today. That was probably what she wanted – to tarry with us as a little dead body. Who'd go straight from ship to ball, fall down dead, and want to be buried straightaway?"

Her husband murmured sympathetically:

"She probably ate something that didn't agree with her and wasn't meaning to die just yet. She didn't seem to complain especially."

"Who was she to complain to? You, Ryazan horseradish, eh?"

"Come off it, silly," her husband said angrily. "I was speaking figuratively, not to make you jealous! Now, lay the table if you've brought anything!"

"Wouldn't you like some sweeties?"

"You and your sweeties, dock-tailed bitch! I want to scoff. Serve up the nosh!"

"Go on, guzzle, who's stopping you?"

"What, am I to gnaw at the plates? The table's empty!"

"Don't get so het up, kamanbat, calm down! You've done enough commanding," Baba Toma tried to reason with him. "There'll be food tomorrow, we haven't got it yet. We're not upper crust, we'll dunk rusks."

"Wretched rusks again, I'm fed up!"

"If you're fed up, you go a-begging. And may you thrive!" Baba Toma sent him on his way Ryazan-fashion. "Else you're a burden to me here, kamanbat. I've had enough of you sat here commanding while I go begging."

Hoping for peace and some kind of dinner, her husband involuntarily softened his tone:

"How can I manage without you? I can't do without my little gingerbread."

But Baba Toma was no longer listening, she had gone to the deceased. She stood at the bed head, closed her friend's eyes and burst into tears.

"You've beat me to it right here, why... more trouble for me."

With these words Baba Toma trod the creaking floorboards to the old wardrobe with the doors that opened painfully stiffly. Fetching a black kerchief, she glanced at her husband's jacket with the tarnished medals. Drawing the curtain across the old, long-unwashed mirror, as is the custom when someone dies, Baba Toma saw her reflection. Wasn't it time for her to die?

"Ah, Dusya, Dusya, you've taken that path, it looks as if it's my turn now. But I'm dooming myself, summoning sorrow, foolish old me. Here you are, Tomachka, black shawl and dead visitor.

Returning to the room, she sadly announced to her kamanbat:

"Dusya there is tired, d'ya think I'm not? Now I'll lie down and die too and then you'll know what it's like without me."

"Who'll give you permission to die, my little gingerbread? Stay nice and sweet and come on, lay the table quick!"

"No!" she said firmly. "I shan't be sweet any more! Life's hard for gingerbreads. And horseradish is no comrade to gingerbread!"

"What can I call you if not gingerbread?" asked the husband. "Who will you be then?"

"I shall be dead tired Baba Toma. It's only you never get tired, Ryazan horseradish, but as you see, gingerbreads do get tired. And even die. I no longer wish for anything, and don't you either!"

Without undressing, she slumped onto the iron bed, which received her tired body with a cold metallic clank.

"What about me?" her husband asked in consternation. "Am I to sit here hungry?"

"Sit – not lie! I'll be here and you go there to her and lean at long last on your love. I have to think about tomorrow and how to raise money: for Dusya for her grave and for you and me for food. Our Duska's suffering is over but you and I, kamanbat, alas, still have orders to live!"

THE JUNKMAN

From the "Old Merv" series of stories

Translated by Richard Govett

It was in the year 1929, or thereabouts, of the last century that a muscleman named Beki moved into our street. He was truly of heroic physique, so he was called Beki-Palvan. My Great Uncle Yanar, may his be the Kingdom of Heaven, used to tell stories about him, always adding that his name in Russian signified Beki the Wrestler, and when this nickname is given to someone who does not take part in wrestling contests, then that signifies that the man is a real strongman.

But Beki, Great Uncle used to say, was heroic in more ways than one. There had never been such a beanpole of a man on our street before or since. And not just on our street but on neighbouring streets too, and maybe in the whole district! And in our parts I never did spy a man matching the description of Beki-Palvan. But don't go imagining that our district is inhabited by pygmies – no, we have our share of lofty folk. Judge for yourself: for example, my Great Uncle Yanar, who told me this story, was taller than me by a head. And as far as stature is concerned, I feel at home even in Sweden, where I now live. And in this country, as you know, people are certainly not deprived of stature.

However, since the days when Beki-Palvan was alive so much time has gone by that many people confuse him with another man from our street. That's Bekgi-Uzyn, which literally means Bekgi-Tall. He was over two metres in stature, but thin as a rake! Was that maybe why he swayed as he walked, like a reed in the water? I remember, as a child, being afraid that one fine day he would be carried off by the wind. But Bekgi-Uzyn lived four decades later than the famous Beki-Palvan, whom we are now talking about.

And so, Beki-Palvan moved into our street in the years of the great economic opportunities, the NEP, or New Economic Policy to be precise. He came here from somewhere and expressed a wish to purchase an ancient homestead. Or rather, what was left of it after two arson attempts and one expropriation – in other words just ruins, as you can imagine.

The local authorities were naturally glad when someone turned up wanting to buy the abandoned homestead. This is what the chairman of the town soviet said to him:

"Pay the money and the homestead's yours! Mind you, that homestead does occasionally go up in flames of its own accord. We are aware of this, so don't be too critical if it burns down just after you've rebuilt it, and your nest-egg's gone for good, ha-ha-ha! Aren't you afraid of that happening?"

Beki-Palvan burst out laughing too:

"What will be will be, and fear never yet saved anyone from death. Don't try and pull my whiskers!"

The chairman of the town soviet scratched the back of his freshly shaven head – a sign that was clearly not in Palvan's favour.

"I hear," he continued, "that you have a pretty wife. Is it worth the risk, buying a house with a curse on it and putting both her and yourself in danger? Young wives, as far as I know, are exceedingly sensitive regarding the loss of their elderly husbands' property. God forbid... Oy, what am I saying, a plague on my tongue! Lenin and Stalin forbid anything like that should suddenly happen to you!

"We'll see..." Beki-Palvan replied. "I'm not one of your sleek tsarist merchants. I'm a seasoned Leninist NEP man. With the new authorities on side and, incidentally, I pursue a very useful business. The country needs junk and it's my business to collect it. I'm a junkman, an arabachi!"

The chairman of the town soviet scratched the back of his head in another display of doubt, and replied with contempt:

"Yes, I know this NEP of yours – it's sheer robbery! But junk, as far as I can judge from these telegrams, is a useful thing." Here he fetched from his desk drawer a sheaf of official papers, threw them on the desk top, picked out the relevant one, tore off a piece and made himself a roll-up from it.

"No-one in our district has had anything to do with this for some while," he continued. "I believe enough trash was collected. So take up the challenge if a beanpole like you doesn't want to go in for anything else. Make the most of it while you can..."

From that day on Beki-Palvan engaged in an occupation unusual for heroes – he toured the town, and nearby villages too, collecting junk. People, children especially, willingly handed him anything they could get their hands on, receiving in exchange some treasured geegaws. These wonders the NEP man brought from faraway Russia. From there he would return always in buoyant mood and in brand new height-of-fashion clothes. At Mary railway station he would hire a luxurious carriage and take a turn round the streets for an hour or two, every now and then opening the carriage door to greet any acquaintances or strangers in a language still little understood in these parts:

"Glory to soviets! Izdrasti! Howdyedoo! Alive, not dead yet? Demn ye all o'ye!"

The people just smiled at the NEP junkman's talk. They liked him speaking like the people, the language of the new regime.

Nevertheless, I cannot vouchsafe that it all happened like that, because it was all long before I was born. And I must say my Great Uncle, while being a great lover of recalling various amazing stories from the past, was not famed for his love of the truth, as far as I can remember. Not for nothing did people who adored hearing his wondrous tales not infrequently call him, but not to his face, an inventor of fables. But at the same time he was not known as a deceiver. Consequently, there was in his stories a fair amount of truth, although no-one can say how much. Anyway, no-one will ever tell you the whole truth about the past!

So my Great Uncle's stories may not be the most inauthentic, especially if you look at the gist of them. In some sense, of course, we all fall victim to various kinds of fabricators, and in this case I come first on the list of them. For I was first to believe my Great Uncle's stories, and here am I retelling them to you. I am doing this to the measure of my talent, but here I must confess I have not a tenth of the mastery which Great Uncle Yanar possessed. He was a God-sent storyteller! It all came naturally to him. He would sit down and just start spinning all sorts of stories! As if he was not making anything up and it was all happening here and now before his eyes! Ah, what a man, although whimsical and petulant at times!

This story, as Yanar related, took place on our street long before you and I were born, and I swear to God it would be a crying shame not to retell it to you. So, this muscleman Beki moved to our street at the very beginning of springtime, selecting for himself the abandoned homestead which on one side looked onto the steppe.

He set to work with some zeal, and began to restore the burnt out ruin. He worked on his own. From his wife, who was called Klavdia, by the way, he received no particular help, as soon became evident to all who lived on our street. She was an unusually fragile and pallid woman. Moreover, by the summertime, when the air would start to be heated in Mary to forty degrees, she would languish from the local temperature so badly that, as neighbours began to remark, she could not think straight: she would try out some song in her native language, or break into laughter and some sort of ditty, in an attempt to raise her husband's spirits or perhaps try to be at least of some help to him, who was grafting for ten. On meeting local folk she liked to repeat:

"It was the devil himself induced me to move here! This is a place to come and die, not live. My first husband used to say: 'In the USSR three holes there be – Termez, Kushka and Mary.' He was speaking the truth!"

In response the people of our street nicknamed her Klava-Halva. There could be no doubt that Klava-Halva was originally an officer's wife. It was surmised that she must have scarpered from a sickly husband and gone off with muscleman, completely miscalculating her powers...

This is the picture of work taking shape on the homestead, according to my Uncle's stories: Beki-Palvan worked like an ox. Having cleared out the courtyard of the homestead, he began to erect the house. He did everything himself and would not let anyone into the homestead. He mixed the clay, fired the bricks and sawed the boards which he brought from the railway depot where, after the tsarist forces, the soldiers of the Red Guard unit were based. And his wife would spend whole days waving a folding fan at her face, sheltering from the heat in the shade of an overhanging vine which had been restored after the arson attacks. Klava-Halva was seen by Atal, her nearest neighbour, more often than anyone. I will repeat his words:

"With a woman like that you don't build, you play hide-and-seek under the blanket!"

But you can say what you like about a beautiful woman. And to hear the gossips on our street, you should never marry at all! One they will call a slut, another the opposite, squeaky clean – also, incidentally, in a defamatory way – and a third they'll call a trollop just because she is alleged to give her husband no rest at night. How do they know all this, everything about everyone? My Great Uncle spoke with perfect logic on this question:

"They're just people! That's what the human tribe is like, I tell you! They make everything their business. Instead of getting down to work and rebuilding some disused house by themselves, they sit in the shade and chatter and pick other folk to pieces."

And, he would go on to reason, so what, if women are extremely imperfect creatures? It's hardly worth while condemning them for that, let alone dying a bachelor. And are we men any better than they? As you see, my Uncle was not someone who would spread gossip about other people's wives, he was just a conscientious storyteller. In his time he had seen and remembered a lot and later, when I was a teenager, in the Sixties of the last century, he would relate it all to me. He wanted me to know what happened in Merv before I was born.

But let us go back and continue the story at the point when the house was completely rebuilt... Yes, just at the point when Klava-Halva ran away from this comfy little nest! Just imagine! Think what it is like when a wife runs away from a living husband, and moreover from one like this strongman! No-one ever expected it of her, even the neighbours and the husband the more so. But alas, in this sublunar world anything you want happens, and what you don't want happens even more often...

It was said that Klava-Halva did not just run away from Beki-Palvan, she did it because she could no longer... Well, you know what I... She could no longer endure his masculine pressure at night! This strongman, if popular rumour is to be believed, had simply taken possession of her because, it was said, he was broad not only in the shoulders and big not only in stature, but in all the other parts of the body, too... Although here, too, I think there was a lot of gossip circulating, because no-one really knew the reason for Klava-Halva's flight. The house was built, but the wife takes flight – did you ever see such a thing? How? Why? For what earthly reason? There was no answer to these questions and so, as I see it, people had to create conjectures, make something up.

One thing is certain, and that is, she did not flee from life's adversities, but something else. People knew that, to please his wife, the junkman had acquired a domestic servant. A lad by the name of Marat from the next street used to dig their kitchen garden, and some young person called Aza, they all decided, who might be originally from the Caucasus, had become completely installed in their house. She cooked and did the washing for the owners of the homestead and also put in order the old carpets and kilims which Beki-Palvan had acquired from the populace for trifles. True, the young and comely Aza was called a distant relative. But this was on account of the fact that the new regime did not permit one to have a servant. Everyone was obliged to work for a *kolkhoz* or the state.

Before she ran away, it is said, Klava-Halva offered him a deal: I'll live, says she, in one part of the house, and you in the other. You come to me once a week, but no more! But, they say, he would not agree, and said:

"I can't do that!"

"So, you can't? Well, then I can't either!"

And so she fled from the house, apparently somewhere very far away. Maybe to Russia, maybe somewhere even further. In search of his wife the strongman travelled to Russia, but returned without the fugitive. It is quite likely she went somewhere further, perhaps even to Pereng. And I can tell you that's not nearby, it's France.

According to my Uncle's story, after Klava-Halva had run away, the junkman simply went out of his mind. He would growl at night like a wounded lion. He was even on the point of planning by his own hand to burn down the cursed homestead – by now for the third and, most likely, last time! Perhaps he might even have done it, were it not for young Aza... The young girl quickly realized that if the house was burned down there would be nowhere for her to go. And she made her none too easy choice and fell passionately in love with the ageing hero. And they settled down in the homestead in love and harmony. But as it turned out, the real tragedy was hereby only delayed for a while, and wait for it...The dark-eyed beauty's love turned out to be not abiding, and the passion transient, which destroyed our strongman. Ah, but I seem to have forgotten to tell you that before Klava-Halva the junkman had another wife – a Turkmen woman, who died in very first childbirth. As it was nothing to do with our street, no-one even knows her name but we are assured that he doted on her and for this reason Beki-Palvan did not care for children to the end of his life. He considered them an aberration of nature, creatures too rumbustious and petulant when young, and when grown-up – ungrateful. Moreover, he thought people should propagate some other way, and leave love just for love, so everything is without deceit and unnecessary tricks! He thought it extraordinarily mean of nature to conceal behind a grand pleasure those fickle little creatures who, on appearing in the world, immediately start to suck the life blood from their parents, so they grow old and go to their graves in no time at all.

But sometimes, as you can judge from his behaviour, he nevertheless missed the company of children. Children were the only outsiders he occasionally allowed into his homestead. He would lavish various trinkets on them and play for them on a primitive whistle. And when he was in the best of all moods he would show them the strength of his famous luxuriant moustache. For this purpose he would insert through the curls of his moustache a fine "*ik*" spindle, with which the girls roll out the little wedding *lepioshki-chelpek* delicacies, and then climb the stairs to the roof and then come down again. He could repeat this trick once or twice or more, but the children were always delighted with the funny but at the same time fascinating show. Incidentally, my Father remembers seeing it when he was only four.

Beki-Palvan settled in with Aza, possessor of the lovely amber eyes, and got on with her even better than with Klava-Halva. For a whole year they lived as one. They could always be seen in an embrace in the daytime, and at night her sweet moans would break out into the steppes, which began just there, over the north fence of the homestead, while from the other side they would float on the sultry air of Old Merv to the ears of the residents of our street. And it seemed as if there was no end to this happiness and never would be.

The beanpole would carry the young Aza in his arms, like a living doll. But one day, apparently, she could not take any more either. "Living doll" likewise found muscleman more than enough. In one year she had become so tired from strongman's mad love that she became tired of life and the black rings never left her eyes. Thinking of running away, she apparently entered into secret relations with Marat, young as a gherkin and, like a gherkin, pimply... Incidentally, it turned out later that he was the nephew of the chairman of the town soviet, the one who was in the habit of scratching the back of his head when he was having serious thoughts about something or suspecting someone of something.

One of the neighbours noticed that, in her husband's absence, Aza would spend hours in the shade of the vine squeezing out the pimples on Marat's face. Later, people decided that it was the pimply fellow who incited her to commit a terrible crime. They saw that as soon as the junkman had left on his cart, this Marat would drop his spade, pull out of his pocket his crumpled *budionovka*, don it at an angle and sneak under the hanging vine. And when the junkman left for Russia the pimply fellow already felt absolute master of the house.

"If only you would love me always!" Aza said to him again and again, kissing his lips and face, which shone with an abundance of youthful passion.

"I promise!" he vowed.

"Only not as strongly as that monster..." she implored.

"Of course, what do you take me for?" he murmured in reply.

Aza was evidently well aware that her husband was no junkman, but a wealthy man who was shrewdly concealing his fortune from the new regime.

She knew that he chose the work of a junkman simply to keep away prying eyes, that not for nothing did he make so many trips to Russia, and that he always returned from there flush with money. She knew, furthermore, that he helped transfer tsarist gold coins and valuables belonging to wealthy Russians fleeing the country via the "eastern corridor" to Iran and Turkey.

It transpires that Aza and her pimply lover agreed to make off with the so-called junkman's entire hoard of gold. And so, once in the dead of night, after a long while of amorous frolics, when Beki-Palvan had succumbed to his wonted deep slumber, Aza got up carefully and fetched the two-edged dagger hidden under the carpet...

Although it must be admitted that no-one, absolutely no-one saw this exactly, it was known almost "for certain" how she plunged the dagger straight into the heart of her serenely sleeping husband. But whether her hand trembled or she was weakened by her long-standing love, but Beki-Palvan refused to die from this blow of the dagger. And she, sure that her deed had been done, went to fetch the junkman's wealth hidden in the brick-built hearth, and was startled to see him in the doorway with the blade sticking out of his chest...

She dropped the gold and the money, and with a scream she ran into the street. Her husband did not lag behind. He chased after her with the dagger stuck in his chest. The wounded husband caught up with his killer-wife already in the street. He seized her firmly by the arm and, drawing from his heart the bloodied dagger, plunged it, still warm, to the very hilt into the heart of his beautiful wife.

All that followed remained on every tongue in our street. The eyewitnesses of that bloody drama later recalled how the couple – the strongman and his young wife – stood embracing for a long time in the street. They said this continued for an eternity, even till the very dawn. No-one dared approach them. It was already growing light when Beki-Palvan at last fell on his knees before her, as if confessing eternal love, and then they collapsed together on the ground. And they lay there as if alive, tightly embracing, when their last sun rose upon them.

In the evening a mighty flame lit up the district... It was the house of Beki-Palvan on fire and no-one here saw Marat again. And not for nothing did the chairman of the town soviet scratch the back of his head. He knew what he was doing.

EGYPTIAN NIGHT OF FEAR

Translated by Richard Govett

Tell me why wanderest thou aimless?
"Egyptian nights"
A.S. Pushkin

In Egypt there grows an amazing cotton of the fluffiest, tenderest kind. Between the rows of the crop you will not find all sorts of stuff preventing you from picking it, underfoot you are not hampered by stinging, clinging weeds such as our cocklebur and branching foxtail. Probably no weeds grow there at all!

Egyptian cotton is the sunniest, smelling of the autumn sunshine! And an Egyptian autumn can be just like ours. Our cotton, too, is drenched in sunshine so powerfully that you are irresistably tempted to snuggle it with your cheek.

I had stopped picking cotton and, straightening up, I glanced at the field and not a soul was to be seen all around. In my flurry of work I seemed to have been cut off from them all, and here I was, standing alone in the middle of a limitless expanse; wherever you looked there was cotton under a massive, hazy sky. It pressed down upon me and underfoot I felt the hot earth. Baking hot. Silence. The voices of the other pickers were barely audible, as if from another planet. Between us was the exhausting noonday heat. Earth began to turn like a dish being spun by someone and the silvery-coppery object was disappearing beyond the horizon. I watched its flight, having collapsed on my side in the sparse shade of the cotton plants between the rows. Even the hard clods of dried clay did not bother my tired body and, drowsy with the noonday Turkmen sun, I closed my eyes.

Had I looked at the sky for too long? I do clearly remember being lured by some mirage which the eye could not glimpse, caught somewhere on the cusp of reality and numinosity.

I did not sleep long, but awoke, arose and left the cotton field. I had a tormenting thirst, but it was checked by the recollection of the water they used to bring us in the fields – warm, heady, dank, with a seaweedy aftertaste, from a rusty cistern which somehow made it taste of blood. At least, that is how it seemed. I had an irresistible desire to drink deep of the true, cool water from a fast-flowing mountain stream and then – to the town! This sudden urge was so strong that I went without second thoughts. There was no point in wondering who could go with me, they were all busy picking cotton.

As soon as the peak season starts, regular bus services between our *kolkhoz* and the town are usually cancelled till the actual October festivities or even the first snow. In these parts the fate of the harvest is being decided all the year round, from morn till night. So you need to hail a passing car to go to town. And that is what I did. I remember only vaguely the driver's face and what we talked about.

...In the afternoon I was walking round the vibrant centre of town, within its beating heart, in the bazaar, where life never stands still. All around was hubbub, tumult and chaos. But I knew that external impressions were deceptive – the life of the bazaar has its own rhythm and its own laws. The traders cry their wares and the customers examine them, value them and bargain. And here was I with them, like someone drugged.

I cannot imagine how I ventured on such a trip. The cotton crop was going to waste in the fields. My peers were enduring back-breaking toil in the fields from dawn till dusk. But here was I in the town, cooling my heels without permission from the *kolkhoz* authorities. How could I get away with it?

But it was too early to fret, I thought. Better make the most of it. I had been lucky, but was wandering quite aimlessly between the rows of stalls amidst the crowd and the crafty traders who would lure any passer-by.

Here was one, pulling me directly by the arm to his counter piled with the finest brocades, exquisite garments from faraway countries, and alongside – mountains of sweetmeats and nuts and coloured phials, probably of musk.

I am delighted and, knowing my subject, immediately inquire:

"Is it Egyptian cotton?"

"Yes," the merchant confirms, placing his hand on his heart. "The lad's guessed correctly. It's all woven of best quality Egyptian cotton. I visit Egypt every month, Cairo itself. There I select the most exquisite wares!

I renew the range of goods more often than anyone, so as to gladden the spirits of my countrymen. They are like my own family. I cannot let them go away disappointed... But you are here for the first time, I haven't seen you here before.

"I will say neverthess," he continues, with a daring glint in his eye which I do not notice at once, "that I like you. You're special. And furthermore handsome and smart and perhaps wealthy, too. If not, no worries, you can get rich if you're smart. I see only one drawback – your clothing. You definitely need to have some garments made from my silks and brocades! The dyes are natural. These fabrics were dyed by the elegant little hands of beautiful Egyptian women working for my master on the Street of the Dyers. Under scorching rays they dissolve the dye in huge vats. Silks and wools just glisten in their clever little hands and the fabric is evenly steeped in the world's most reliable dyes made from the roots and petals of wild plants. The colours of these flowers are not to be found even in the rainbow.

"Oh, what beauties they are, my lad! If only you could see them just once with your own eyes! In their eyes is the latent fire of love, their tender faces are hidden from the burning sun beneath the veil. Oh my lad, you should see these beauties and fall in love with one, then you could accompany me there every month!"

The next moment I see I am standing somewhere between the stalls with a length of precious brocade in my hands, and the people of the bazaar are scurrying around me. No-one takes any notice of me. I now realize I am stuck not only without money for dinner but without my meagre savings. Missing dinner is a small worry, but how am I to get back? How will I get home?

I should discuss this with the trader in Egyptian fabrics. But he no longer wants anything to do with me. He is holding another customer by the arm, pompously extolling his wares. He does not want to know me, and sternly declares:

"Don't interfere, lad, I'm serving! You've got a bargain there! Make way for the other customers! I can't look after just you all day. The bazaar day is short, you can hardly blink an eye, and it's evening and then night..."

Yes, he's quite right, this seller of Egyptian wares, and he smells nice. The days of autumn are not long, and soon the golden scarab beetle in the sky will fade and I have not even had time for dinner, to drink of that fragrant green tea, accompanied by sultanas or dried apricots brought here from cool mountain valleys somewhere half-way on the route from the delta of the fabulous Nile.

***

Then I remembered I had not had time to wash. And surely, after a day in town it is a shame not to call at the bath-house. It is always refreshing and oh! how I needed to wash away the unpleasant smell after dealing with that deceitful shopkeeper and his fake brocades. So I wandered to where, in the shade of some elm trees there was concealed a squat, ancient hammam which had washed Asiatic folk for centuries.

A bath is the *kolkhoznik's* dream. In the fields I would dream about it no less than about fine foods. Here I was wending my way there through the narrow lanes of Old Merv in the scorching September sun with that stupid length of brocade under my arm. I plodded up to the rather gloomy building with its massive wooden doors, scrutinized the time-blackened unintelligible carved patterns, motivated either by an excessive curiosity or irritated by the itchy dust.

I was not lucky straightaway, because I had to wait my turn with others craving the blessings of the bath. It was said that even in earlier times the hammam could not accommodate simultaneously all those who wanted to wash. At any rate, as our slant-eyed history teacher, who had a precise knowledge of everything, would lecture us in his monotonous, lulling voice, this hammam used to serve the mediaeval caravans passing this way on the Silk Road from East to West and, of course, on the return journey...

I sat in the waiting area till someone should emerge from the depths of the building leaving room for me. So I thought it a good sign when, to my surprise, I was approached by this stranger, who displayed a pleasing friendliness towards me, smiling at first reticently and then with the whole breadth of his smoke-stained teeth. Without letting me recover from my first pleasant impression, the stranger immediately wanted to know if I really wanted a bath. Understandably, I replied in the affirmative, perhaps a little light-heartedly but with complete circumspection. I said:

"Yes, of course, Sir, but how else? surely one goes to the bath-house to have a bath, otherwise what is the point in coming here?"

Here the stranger nodded as if in agreement with me but, as I realized, only out of emphasized politeness and urbane courtesy. Then, without hesitating for long, he added:

"If you wish not only to take a bath but also to receive the deepest enjoyment from the hammam, don't be shy, just say the word and I'll be able to arrange it for you."

My heart gave a thump – here was the long-awaited moment! The untold mystery of transient earthly happiness to come! Is it not for this we are from the very first born on earth, toil by the sweat of our brow in the *kolkhoz* fields, some of us deep underground in stifling coalmines where everyone has a constant need for a drink? Hey! what is it like to want a drink, to be tormented by thirst... and suddenly feel, out of the blue, a sweet moment of happiness? Anyway, it seemed to be my turn, and naturally I was agreeable. But I was worried about one thing – that I was being summoned into the distant unknown not by a nymph-like beauty clad in exotic translucent silks, but by a man – smiling, yes, and soft-spoken – but ungainly and furthermore dark-complexioned such as you might not meet even among the Egyptians.

Only then did it occur to me that the man was in fact from Egypt or visited there frequently with the merchant caravans. For surely only in distant countries where eternal summer reigns could a person be sunburnt to such a degree as to babble unblushingly of the devil knows what! I thought for a moment as if looking into water and reading my fortune reflected there.

The stranger gave a canny smile, only to suddenly burst into tears. Then he began to reassure me:

"Don't think badly of me, my lad. I just need help..."

How did this man with yellow teeth know I was the sympathetic kind? That it was in my nature to help those in distress? No, this man was no simpleton, he might have been observing me from that very morning when I came to the bazaar. Such things were said to happen. I was truly of a sympathetic nature and understandably my character could not change in an instant at the very first encounter with danger. I answered him thus:

"Tell me, Sir, what you need, and I will try and help you to the best of my ability. In any case, I will not leave you in your distress."

Then he quietly dried his tears and expressed himself more explicitly:

"Let's go to the woom," he said, slurring his words in his excitement. "And there I'll tell you everyfing foroughly. No-one will disturb us dere. A whole hour..."

I soon came to from my daydream on again hearing the stranger's repulsive way of speaking. He spouted such filth my ears burned no less than in the hammam, conveying what we teenagers from the *kolkhoz* fields only occasionally encountered in the ghastliest horrors and so long after the event that they seemed to date from the time of the mediaeval caravans.

And now I was assailed as if by the scalding steam of the hammam! I was instantly reminded of the story of my chum Kadysh and what happened latterly to his distant relative. He allegedly came to this bath-house and, without sensing any danger, began to strip naked like all the others – and where would a *kolkhoznik* strip naked if not in the bath? For some reason, at that precise moment there were few people in the bath, maybe none at all, except an ugly old man sitting there, calmly watching the lad till he was left as naked as the day he was born. And then the old man went up to him and, as if checking a crystal vase for sound, flicked the boy's dangle, quietly concealed between his legs, and said: "Come, lad, with me to a separate room." And he added, without batting an eyelid, that he would make in an hour a sum of money you could not earn even if you picked the total crop of cotton in the whole *kolkhoz* field on your own!

Kadysh's relative revealed that he fled into the street without his trousers. And in an instant I found myself in the almost empty street with the heavenly luminary still scorching mercilessly. There I was pursued by a farewell from that habitué of the dark hammam:

"Wretched cotton-fucker!" he spat after me.

I stood there in the burning Turkmen sunshine, shivering as if I had just climbed out of an ice hole. Horror carried my feet through the narrow, meandering lanes. I ran, stumbling and falling, and the hammam chased me all the way to the bazaar. There people were walking about as if nothing had happened, totally unaware of what was going on under their very noses! But what can you expect of bazaar folk? They have been as thoughtless as that from time immemorial! Slipping into the crowd, I calm down and forget about myself and time and how quietly it flows.

***

How long have I been wandering round the bazaar, if the golden scarab is already growing dim and beginning to descend from the heavens by those golden threads to hide at night behind the highest *barkhans*? The bazaar folk are no longer bustling between the rows as at noon, the last customers are hurriedly bargaining with the purveyors of various victuals, sweetmeats and vegetables, hastening to fill their baskets and quickly make for home. The traders are putting away their unsold wares into sacks and crates without ceasing to praise them.

There are quite a few cunning practical jokers around who gain real pleasure from twisting some simpleton round their little finger. If they succeed, you must see with what delight such a joker heads homeward, humming into his moustache, whistling with a subtle play of the eyebrows.

But who is to fret, if not I? I have been without food for so long I can no longer make out who I am, what I am doing and why I have found myself in the bazaar. Who was that merchant who flattered me with his cloying speeches and sold me some fabric which, while not of poor quality, obviously was not Egyptian? Why did I decide to waste all my savings on that trash? Tomorrow, with the first rays of the sun, I must be in the cotton field, but how and on what am I to get home?

Tired out, head down, I trudge from the bazaar in the wake of the last customers and traders. A man overtakes me accompanied by an unbearably delicious smell. As he walks, he puts into his mouth huge steaming hot *manti* and, catching my hungry look, he turns to me.

"Young lad, what's wrong? haven't you eaten since morning?" he asks in surprise. "Have a taste, these *manti* are the most scrumptious in the bazaar! I always buy them from the same woman. You can trust her, she sells meat and not just anything that comes to hand, like some people. In this bazaar you mustn't trust anyone you bump into. There are all types here. They'll twist you round their little finger, they'll fleece you, they'll fool you so you'll never guess how cruelly you've been deceived!"

The *manti* are really delicious, two of them, they melt in the mouth, they go straight down I'm so hungry. I eat greedily, forgetting all decencies.

"Don't be shy, lad. Don't be shy," my unexpected benefactor says encouragingly, and laughs. "I guarantee they're not from human flesh!"

The food sticks in my throat, I retch, spewing out what I have not managed to swallow, and raise my frightened eyes to him. He grins broadly and confidingly takes me by the sleeve.

"Don't worry, I was joking. How could there be human flesh at the bazaar? They only sell beef and lamb here, and occasionally wild game which you can shoot in the Turanian forests and upper reaches of the river.

"Where are you headed for? I can drive you somewhere if you like, and you can pay a reasonable price. I have enough money, I value friendship more than cash or even gold. So keep up with me, get in the car and tell me where you want to go. I see you're not local. You're rural, from somewhere out in the sticks. How did you get here? You probably don't know the strict rules of this bazaar... It's already late, it'll soon be night, so don't turn your nose up at my offer, there won't be any others."

We come to his little old auto and I can see a woman and someone in a turban already seated in the car.

"Oh," my travelling companion exclaims. "My regular clients are already here, they've let themselves into the car and are waiting for me! Come on, you get in too, and make yourself comfortable. We'll drop them off first and then take you home."

I don't have time to open my mouth, no-one asks me. I want to offer some objection but instead catch myself smiling stupidly. I see myself as if from one side and do not even have time to be surprised at this feeling that has got into me from God knows where. Oh what a town, seething with fiends and villainy! Pot of filth! Where now is that swindler merchant who twisted me round his little finger and cleaned me out? He's probably sitting at home on his shady veranda, sipping fragrant green tea and smugly smiling at his wife, boasting, the little spider, of his day's successes. And I'm travelling in some battered jalopy towards the gathering twilight – whither, why and with whom?

"Excuse me, where are we going?" I probe and peer at the street through the dirty, dim, long-unwashed window.

"Couldn't you drop me off first and then take the woman and the venerable gentleman in the turban?" I plead.

"No haste, my lad, everything in due course!" the driver frowns. "I can't offend my regular clients for some bird-of-passage finding himself in the bazaar maybe for the first and last time."

He exchanges glances with the traders and I catch a long, mean look from the person seated alongside. He just cannot stop squinting at me and smirks as if to say it's all quite true and the lad is hardly likely to find himself in the bazaar a second time.

The woman is silent throughout the journey, but the darker the streets the more often I catch her strange look at me. The mysterious glint in her eyes frightens me. I try to make out how I have suddenly found myself between her and her travelling companion in the turban, but to no avail.

We drive a long way and outside the car's dirty windows the dark, dark mare night has long been galloping unceasingly. She is really more blue-black...

The darkness all around looks alive. I can even hear the clatter of hooves and the breathing of the mare alongside, as if she is trying to warn me of some kind of conspiracy.

One moment she is running far ahead, lost in the feeble light of the headlamps, and the next she is submissively running behind us. The car has for a long time been rattling along dark, unknown country roads, giving us no chance of discerning our whereabouts. We are driving through wild country; there is no oncoming traffic and not a single human being; only the phosphorescent eyes of the occasional fox gleam and blink in the darkness. The pit of my stomach sinks, my belly churns, and I feel with my whole being that this is an unsavoury business. We're on the road to Hell!

"We're here," the driver announces, as if guessing my alarm. "If I am not mistaken, this is your destination, isn't it, my dear fellow?" he says to the old man. "Or do you wish to get nearer?"

"You all wait for me here," the other responds gruffly, climbing out of the car. "You can come up a bit later if you like," he calls out to the driver already from the darkness. Then he comes back and orders his woman companion: "You stay with the lad today!"

The three of us remain in the car, where an oppressive silence reigns. The driver's jocular mood has disappeared somewhere. I feel all over the tension growing in him minute by minute. Not for the good, I note to myself... My heart feels crushed by an ugly premonition. The driver pays me no attention. Several minutes pass, then half an hour, an hour, and still no sign of our fellow-passenger.

It's stuffy. We sit in silence, listening to the click of the steppeland cicadas, the howling of the jackals at the lazy moon. Sounds of other incomprehensible and mysterious nocturnal creatures. At length, the driver gets out and goes in search of his client, forbidding me to leave the car. Once again, the time drags: a minute, half an hour, an hour, more..

My fellow travellers seem to have melted into the night, except for the woman, who is piercing me ever deeper with her strange gaze. What can I do?

I have not come to a decision when I feel the woman's hot breath right above my ear:

"Boy, you're doubtless very little, are you? Have I guessed right?" she says, taking me by the hand and drawing me close, and her breasts are like clumps of earth firmed after watering.

"Tell me, have I guessed right?" she torments me further.

The car shakes with her languid but unkind laughter. She is so strong! With difficulty I break out of the car and go in search of my fellow travellers.

After a few paces I discover a cemetery enclosure with dark tombs concealed beyond. Oh God! Oh heavenly powers! Where have they brought me? Do they really want to sacrifice me to idols of some sort? In our districts there have ever abounded rumours and legends about secret sacrifices. For centuries people have disappeared in these places, but of late it has been mainly trusting children and teenagers who might get into someone else's car, as has now happened to me...

The thought of running away flashes through my mind, but my legs, as if benumbed, won't obey me. As if under hypnosis, I go further into the depths of the dark cemetery, roaming among the ancient tombs, not yet losing hope of finding my mysterious companions.

They are nowhere. The moon is no help, it is on the wane. Its meagre light leaves everything around almost indiscernable. And as if to spite me, it is hiding behind stormclouds. Now you cannot see a thing – total black-out! I almost grope my way forward, my eyes gradually become accustomed to the darkness, and somewhere over in a far corner of the cemetery I notice the dark silhouettes of people. As if bewitched, I go thither on my benumbed legs. My path is endlessly long, I stumble on old graves, fall and get up again. Finally, I find myself behind the backs of my accidental fellow travellers, who are, oh my God! – sitting by a dug grave, and before them on a spread shroud lies dark a full-length corpse! My mind refuses to accept what is happening, I cannot believe my eyes. I go closer and strain my eyes in the hope of making sure I am mistaken, that it's all a hallucination, for such a thing just cannot be!

Just then the moon peeps out from behind the black stormclouds and lifts out of the darkness the silhouettes of my travelling companions. Their faces are bloody and they are tearing pieces of dead man's flesh from the body of the deceased and dispatching them into the dark recesses of their mouths. As if at a command they simultaneously turn to me and the merchant and the driver both have a black liquid running out of their mouths. Their arms are covered in blood up to the elbows and what's more... My companions have no faces at all! They are faceless! Where have their faces gone? Oh, Tangry! Oh, Heaven help us! Help He-e-elp!

I scream out loud, I try with all my might to run away, but my legs will not obey me. I stumble and fall, I try to run and fall again, but the cannibals are gaining on me... He-e-lp!

I scream with a terrible sound, I fall on the nearest grave, I hit my head painfully on the edge of it, and I wake up. I open my eyes...

All around a strange silence reigns. Only a bee is buzzing above my ear. Or a wasp perhaps? Just in case, I try not to make any sudden movement. I listen. Where am I, what's the matter with me? Gradually, as if in slow motion, my memory comes back. I recall how I fell asleep, exhausted by the noonday heat. Now, judging by the sun's reddish rays obliquely descending on the limitless rows of cotton, it is nearly dusk. The balminess before evening...

So I haven't been awake? I haven't been to the bazaar? I didn't buy the brocade from the dealer in Egyptian wares? And I didn't get in the car with the stranger? I didn't meet the corpse-eaters? I carefully feel in my pocket. If the money I earned is still there, that means nothing happened... With relief I discover at the bottom of my pocket the little coins – my scant earnings.

That's it! I dreamt this whole horror! It was a dream! But I don't make a habit of just lying down and going to sleep in the middle of a working day! I must have had sunstroke and lost consciousness. Yes, for so long that I had time to take a trip to town and come back.

I jump up and what do I see? The cotton pickers are already filing towards the lorry at the edge of the field. They chuck their sacks onto the lorry and then one after another they clamber onto the vehicle, laden to the top, and perch on the sacks in flocks like rooks. At the field station they will hand in the crop they have gathered for the day. And then they will go home in time to get enough sleep till sunrise tomorrow. But before bed they are bound to watch TV to find out which *kolkhoz* has raced ahead in the cotton harvest, and how *kolkhozniks* can keep the money they have earned safe, so it does not get into the hands of thieves and fraudsters.

Obviously, to make sure this does not happen, better not go to the bazaar – it's no place for honest folk. Our type don't go there. At the bazaar there are so many insidious pitfalls lying in wait for the *kolkhoznik* that it's better for them never to set foot there! Or was it only I who met with so many opportunist hoaxers and insidious, swindling traders? Perhaps...

Beyond the distant *barkhans* where, having completed his daily journey, the beetle-scarab, now inflated to fantastic proportions, has descended to spend the night, sunset has inflamed the sky. The song of the larks occasionally merges with the voices of girls walking in flocks to the edge of the field, some traipsing along the ground, others bearing on their shoulders the tightly filled sacks of cotton. But the golden scarab, casting earthwards the last sheaves of now purple threads, seems to be calling: Does anyone wish to climb these threads straight up to me in the heavens?

A moment, while I choose my path. But earthly life with its heavy burdens and weariness draws one to herself and the laughter of the tired but resilient girls lures me ever more powerfully. I obediently follow them and, shouldering a heavy load of *kolkhoz* wealth, I head towards where, at any moment now, the huge red luminary will be extinguished.

ON THE EDGE

Translated by Richard Govett

One autumn night, on the edge of a huge city, a weary dog trotted along a dark pathway, stopping now and then to look into the rubbish pits and sniff at them. He was searching for food. At last, his canine sense of smell caught among the rotting filth the whiff of a recently discarded bone. The dog began to tremble all over. Without taking his eyes from the desired delicacy, Alabay ran around the pit several times. He could not wait to get at the bone.

In the places familiar to him there remained no courtyard he had not sniffed around, no rubbish tip he had not ransacked and no waste water pit he had not investigated. He had not been lucky, for others had managed to seize what could have assuaged his hunger if only for a while. Old Alabay was last at the dogs' dinner table. His stronger cousins behaved more and more self-confidently and cheekily on his own territory and his chances of survival were ever diminishing. And so the pedigree wolfhound had to rummage among the waste water pits like the hindmost mongrel. But was it so long ago that on these streets whole packs of strays held veritable dogs' banquets around the rich rubbish tips? Then there was more strength to his paws, then he would fight to the death with impetuous hounds not for a bone but for the odd bitch – at all costs to avoid losing her or letting someone else get her. Then he did not know what on earth hunger was. He remembered clearly – that's how it was! Now for three days and three nights his empty stomach had been twisting and turning like a spindle. Precisely his stomach and no other part of his tormented body. Now he had to think about survival, how not to die of hunger! Many of his days had passed into oblivion in waiting for someone to throw into the pit some leftover meat or at least a bone. Hunger had so penetrated his brain and overcome his old body that he was left with nothing but the feeling of permanent emptiness in his stomach and memories of the house on the edge of the precipice where he was born.

Having performed the dance of hunger around the pit, the dog started crawling towards his cherished goal and soon a third of his body was hanging over the pit. He crept a little further – the great lump of bone was now alongside and he turned his ungainly neck and tried to reach it with his jaws. No use! It was all in vain! Now his body was suspended dangerously over the pit, and although his huge head was over the ill-starred bone, he did not manage to grab it. He whimpered helplessly and twitched his abbreviated ears. The sheep's rib was not so hopelessly far away. The dog's imagination became more and more excited. A bone with meat on it! Alabay could not tear his greedy eyes from it, its intoxicating smell put all his innards into action and he drooled at the mouth. In desperation Alabay would have leapt into the stinking viscosity, but he carefully crept back. Fear of the pit had been deeply instilled into him from puppyhood. It could swallow you whole like a gnawed bone and chew you up like a tasty morsel.

***

In the dog's dim memory there began to emerge living pictures of many years ago, when they were a whole pack of seven carefree puppies, fighting on any pretext or none and suckled by the caring and loving bitch, Big White, winner of many of the veritable dog battles which were organized by the people living there. It was on one of those happy, carefree days that they suffered the first loss in their big canine family. This is how it happened… Having dozed as usual after feeding her offspring, the mother slowly got up and went in search of food for herself. The puppies scrambled after her through the mud house entrance. Like multicoloured balls of fluff they ran in different directions in a world lit by a high, generous sun, and came across something incomprehensible – before them appeared a pit. Other smells, different from that of mother's milk, aroused their interest. Snow White went nearer the edge. The pit squeaked desperately like a puppy and then squelched and went quiet... Mother made long, unsuccessful searches for her lost puppy and then, tired and resentful, for the first time fed them milk that was tasteless and bitter from grief.

Alabay lost all patience and continued to circle the pit. Absorbed in the hunt for inaccessible food, he was nearly caught under the wheels of a lorry growling its way up the street which was empty at that hour. He ran to the curb and started licking his paws which only by sheer chance had not been crushed. His head was dizzy from hunger and his past started coming to life in his imagination.

***

At first the mud house where they lived was their dog's paradise. Through the high window with its smashed panes and through the hole in the thin clay wall the sun's rays swept over the broken wooden butt with handle-less dipper sprawled behind the smoke-blackened door and the ragged home-woven hangings – everything the puppies had inherited from the former owners. It was evident from everything that the people had gone off somewhere in a hurry, without even taking their pregnant bitch with them. They had evidently tried to peel from the door and take with them at least a cutting from a newspaper about the bitch, winner of her breed, but were unable to, and the piece of paper fluttered in the slightest breeze, waving goodbye to the owners who had long ago disappeared. But mother and they were happy and warm there.

But then they got to know real life, rough and uncivil. In the first two months Skewbald lost one of his brothers, Snow White. Then came the next disaster: the puppies broke into someone's kitchen garden, forgetting about the danger, and romped in the flowering clover among the multicoloured butterflies and the dragonflies with their funny bulging eyes. They managed to trample the clover and work up a good appetite. It was time to go home, but then a boy appeared. He took his trousers down and started to pee. Skewbald was first to rush at him, barking and inviting him to play. But the boy let out a terrible roar and retreated. Holding his trousers with one hand, he darted into the house. A puny chap with an evil expression rushed out. Gathering stones as he went, he started throwing them into the stirring clover. The puppies scattered and ran into their hovel. Their pursuer barred the exit and the puppies started hastily burrowing into the straw. But the terrible stranger had seen where they lived and as soon as he was gone Big White's offspring forgot all about him.

Next morning, as soon as their mother had disappeared through the bright opening in the wall, that Puny of the day before appeared there carrying a sack. He picked up the puppies by the ears from under the straw where they had tried to hide and shoved them in the sack with a chuckle.

But his loud laughter ceased when Black Brow bit him on the finger. Puny howled in pain like a dog and sat on his haunches. Then he jumped up and looked around angrily. He seized the broken dipper and giving it a mighty swing beat Black Brow on his fluffy little head. He took the softened puppy carefully by the ears and in disgust chucked him into the darkness where the others were huddled. Only Skewbald was left. Puny tried to catch the puppy by the neck but realised he could get bitten again. He spat loudly.

"We'll meet again somehow, pup!" he grunted angrily.

Little Skewbald could not calm down for ages and just stood there, bristling, till mother appeared in the hole in the wall through which Puny had disappeared with the sack on his back. That evening she would go and come back many times, listening to every rustle behind the thin walls of the mud house. Only late that night would she lie down on the earthen floor. The furious bloodhound bitch howled right through till morning. And at dawn they both left their native hovel for good. When he was grown up, Alabay only once ventured there, but of the dwelling not a trace was left. Rows of huge multi-storey marble monstrosities had risen up from the direction of the city, encroaching more and more on the very edge of the ravine...

No-one knows what his destiny would have been, had he ended up in the sack with the other puppies. He had lived in dire straits to the point of exhaustion, traipsing along numerous roads many times over, day and night exploring endless rows of courtyards in search of food which more often than not would assuage his continual hunger only for a while, but to this day he had never met any of his brothers and sisters. But no, there was one such instance in his life. He remembered, because of the eternal companion of his freedom and unlimited independence – that cursed hunger, which had pursued him all these years, he unexpectedly wandered into some courtyard... In the far corner of the courtyard he saw a bowl, full of food. An unexpected gladness bathed his heart. In the twinkling of a eye he pulled a big meaty bone out of the bowl, but just then, clanging his iron chain, there appeared a huge dog who bared his teeth and rushed at him. Alabay was rooted to the spot. He could not take one step or make one sudden movement, nor did he try to do anything. No, he was not afraid, he did not flinch at the sudden, impetuous attack by his well-fed rival. Not in the least. He recognised the family smell. That arrogant, unruly dog was his own brother whom Puny had first stunned and then taken away in a sack. Kidnapped Black Brow! And he seemed to recognise his brother, he must have, how could he not have? But with what grimness and hatred he rushed at Skewbald! Alabay refused to believe that his brother wanted to fight him. What's more, he greeted him with a snarl and again tried to grab that bone, the meaty one. But Black Brow attacked with the same ferocity. He would not think of letting him near the bowl of food, although it was obvious he was not dying of hunger.

Alabay went away hungry and bitter. He suddenly hated the loyal servant of a cruel person who had once mercilessly destroyed their doggy home. Naturally, his hunger was blunted by the following day, but he never forgot the insult meted out to him by his own brother, who had now become a slave. The pain would not go away, and he was reminded of it constantly on any pretext. His brother Black Brow was serving the one who once deprived them of their family happiness – it was impossible to forget that.

Suddenly some floppy-eared dog emerged from the darkness and made straight for "his" – Alabay's – waste water pit. Alabay's eyes let him down – how did they not notice his rival in time? A life of hunger, endless journeys in search of food, the suffering, the cruel fights with cousins – all this had obviously made him old before his time, had loosened his teeth, weakened his claws and had of course blunted the sharpness of his eyesight. The newcomer began circling the waste water pit. Alabay realized he was salivating, in vain. But having come on the off-chance he was hoping for something and tried to stretch out his paw to reach the bone at the bottom of the pit, as if he were not a dog but a cunning fox or jackal! His efforts were now worrying Alabay, and he got up slowly, approached the edge of the pit and cast a proprietorial eye at the bottom of the pit – the bone still lay there. He sniffed to make sure. Floppy-Ears did not like that and he snarled spitefully and started launching himself at Alabay. The cock-a-hoop behaviour of the unexpected rival enraged the wolfhound. He responded with a snarl, as if to warn the mischief-maker:

"Get back or it'll be the worse for you!"

But the rival was looking for trouble. Alabay felt his chest muscles stiffen and his teeth protrude. Floppy-Ears had no intention of retreating, not at all, he was seeking an opportunity to make the first attack. Finally, making a quick turn around his opponent, he seized him by a front paw and immediately closed his teeth, causing Alabay a sharp pain. Alabay panicked for just a moment and then nimbly seized the offender by the scruff of his neck, tightly closed his mighty jaws and started shaking him. The rival immediately relaxed his hold and, whining piteously, tried to break free. Before letting Floppy-Ears go, Alabay swung him several times to and fro by his neck. When at last Alabay opened his jaws, Floppy-Ears took to his heels, whining and whimpering like a year-old puppy.

The wolfhound returned to the edge of the pit and lay down in his former place, once more making sure that the bone was in the pit. He remembered that his mother, Big White, had also once had to fight with just such a malign dog. It happened when there were just the two of them left, and mother was prepared to tear to pieces anyone who dared harm her surviving puppy. One such did turn up, fell upon him and started throttling him. Big White arrived just in time, otherwise he could have had his throat wrung literally in a moment. That is how puppies are killed – by the fangs of jealous adult dogs. Mother managed to stand up for Skewbald. But a few days later a band of children happened to catch the puppy in a courtyard and subjected him to a cruel ritual. They trimmed his ears and tail with a razor blade and no one came to his aid. Mother ran around grunting, not daring to attack the boys, not because she was afraid but because she had not been taught to attack people. She wagged the stump of her tail and pricked up her trimmed ears – a true sign in these parts that the bitch was initially domestic and not stray. The children pointed at the bleeding, frightened puppy, crying:

"Alabay! Alabay!"

And so, by losing the ends of his tail and ears, the puppy instantly acquired his nickname. And so, quite accidentally, Skewbald stood out in the herd of strays and became like an ordinary, domestic dog. Then he often heard his nickname being called out by the young boys and gradually began to recognize it.

Alabay did not like street dogs because they were hot tempered and liked to fight. But he and his mother very soon found themselves in the very centre of these bloody quarrels. At the beginning of their independence a veritable battle of dogs broke out on the outskirts of the city. The stray dogs gathered in whole packs for some reason or for division of territory. He remembered feeling as if he, still a puppy, had teeth starting to lengthen of their own accord and protrude and he was inflamed with a desire to try them out for real. When grown-up dogs started frenziedly tearing each other's fur, seized each other's ears and sank battle-tempered fangs into the bodies of their enemies, and crunched each other's necks, he started to growl with fear, assaulting and biting everything that lay around – sticks, branches of trees, even an old boot – in fact, anything his teeth could cope with then! That was how he satisfied the blood flowing copiously to his gums – blood which required an outlet. The more he wanted to help mother, the tighter and tighter his jaws clamped together. Big White was still in the centre of this fierce battle. Sometimes she would emerge for a moment from the dense tangle of dogs tearing each other to pieces, but then she would again throw herself into the very thick of the battle. Her expression was that of someone who had fought against everyone all on her own. For him, the end of the battle was as incomprehensible as its beginning. The stray dogs, in ones or twos, some bleeding, some on three legs, some on two, started leaving the battlefield. They all left, including the mortally wounded ones. They took their death with them and lived with it for a few days in solitude. Big White also left the battle. Nobody even thought of chasing her. There were probably none of her enemies among the fighters.

After that incident, the dog gradually, with each passing month, began to keep apart from mother. He quickly learned from new impressions. He could not wait to become a grown-up, to rely only on his own young paws and fangs. Life with mother had become boring. Big White no longer took care of him as before, and gave him as much liberty as he could take. Soon she cooled towards him altogether and fell out of his life for a long time. Only once, with the onset of the third springtime of their parting, he noticed her in another pack. On seeing his mother, he forgot about everything for a moment and bounded up to her like a little puppy! But Big White did not show him special attention, sniffed him all over and went away. The male dogs from her pack started growling impolitely... He realized that if he ignored the warning, it would not end happily for him, there would be a fight. So there was nothing for it but for him to retire. This time he parted with mother forever.

***

Now he had become old and feeble. His teeth were not up to even the easiest prey. In his best years he would have fetched that accursed bone from the bottom of the waste water pit with what was then his accustomed light double-kicking leap! But now he did not have the strength for that sort of thing. No doubt, from now on he would have to content himself with others' leftovers. Nothing could be changed. Even his half-brother, fed, like him, with Great White's milk, would not share his food with him and chased him away from his full bowl. So what could he expect from other, strange dogs?

The heaviness in his body grew and poisoned the air he breathed, burdened his lungs and penetrated together with his meagre food into his stomach. Something incomprehensible and unknown lodged in all his old wounds and pursued him day and night. Is that not death? With a feeling of dumb instinct he guessed that the length of the roads he had left to cover was not great. But that was not what unsettled him. The most important thing was that he wanted to live out the rest of his life as he wished: without taking food from the weak and without being humiliated by the stronger and more successful. He lay, resting his head on his weary paws. Now he could lie more often and longer than usual, he could lie for whole days and nights at a time. The damp earth drew him to itself more than life did. Were it not for hunger, he would have stayed on the same spot until he had transferred to the damp earth all the remaining heat of his decrepit body. But hunger kept reminding him that he was still alive and would have to look for food all the same. With the same ease with which he dispatched a bone into his muzzle, that cursed hunger would rouse him every morning, put him on his paws and chase him in search of sustenance till late at night. And now it was all finished! There it was, his last objective, melting at the bottom of the pit – an objective he was no longer fit enough to retrieve!

The dog lay on the rim, looking sadly into the darkness. The events entering and leaving his memory were confused and disorderly, and his memory did not remain fixed on anything for long. But he would never forget how he was humiliated by his own brother in the courtyard of Puny's home. And this evening it again came to mind. Skewbald Alabay recalled it once more. Why did his brother behave like that? Did Puny feed him badly? Not likely, he was replete! But could his brother have been reincarnated as someone else? What happened there was for him the most disgusting humiliation in all his canine life. Memories of that day pressed on his heart and made his head ache. He was practically whining from the pain and vexation. But his shaggy head still lay motionless on his front paws.

The cockerels living on the outskirts solemnly crowed midnight. In this part of the city, more like a province than a capital, the lights had long ago been extinguished in the windows of the row of brick houses huddled close together. Night pressed in. The people had left the streets to wandering animals, insects and other nocturnal beings and were lost in deep sleep in their homes.

At that moment someone suddenly appeared in the darkness. He was walking like a homeless man – or had he been thrown out of his home into the night? He was going up the street towards the place where the last vehicle had passed by a little earlier. A noisy, stinking vehicle. Alabay first noticed the silhouette and then observed that it was moving and getting bigger, approaching. Gradually "something vague" was transformed into a person. Now the dog could hear his uneven, nervous steps. Catching the human scent, Alabay realised that the passer-by was afraid, and so he instinctively growled. The person shied to one side and picked up a weighty stone and flung it at him. Its flight was broken by the dog's left flank. The wolfhound instantaneously jumped up. He hesitated for just a second from the pain and then, leaping over the waste water pit, he launched himself at the careless benighted stranger. If he had caught up with him the man would have been the worse for it. He realised this in time and dashed into the first convenient courtyard. The dog barked at him as is proper and then moved away. He no longer doubted where he should go, and made straight for the place where his half brother Black Brow still lived with the long clanking chain round his neck. Alabay had thought of something – not today, but long ago, perhaps on the day when they had clashed for the first time after being parted for so many years. He wanted to save his brother from bondage, from the prison of humiliation. Black Brow had been the least lucky of the seven. It was his cruel lot to serve his arch enemy. Hapless one, apart from Alabay there was no-one to help him. Skewbald was the last of Big White's family who was free. No, he could not leave his brother in the lurch, although he himself had only very little life left in reserve. He must not delay.

Alabay ran forward without a pause. He had passed several small side-streets, had taken the narrowest street in the direction of the mountains, and finally turned into a broad, well-lit road. He knew this road well. Although it had not a single rubbish pit, mongrels were constantly roaming here, because there was always something to live off at the back of a row of shops. This road reminded him of a multitude of ripped off or chewed ears and tails, maimed paws, broken ribs and gnawed dewlaps. He had been here quite often, but now he was indifferent to the smells, although his hunger made itself felt with sharp pangs in his stomach. The dog tried to ignore them. He would run along the bright road to the little bazaar on the left-hand side of the road, go past it and ascend a little way to an old garden, and at its exit he would turn onto the last, well-lit street along which he would have to run until his paws were tired. Further on, in the direction of the mountains, there would be narrow, sinuous streets of single-storey brick and clay alternately. There he would have to seek the courtyard of that man.

He ran and ran until he forgot about his tiredness. At length he stopped on one of the darkest streets. He looked around. Checking something for himself, he sniffed the roadside trees and ran on a little. There it was – that same fork. If he continued up the street it would lead to the edge of the ravine, and if he went to the right, to that memorable courtyard. He stopped for a little. He howled gently and chose the first way, reaching the very edge of the city. Beyond the last house, standing on the edge of the ravine, he turned back from a high hill. The city lay far below. Thousands of different coloured lamps burned like cold stars, impassionately and indifferently. The dog's eyes did not rest on them, but rose higher, towards a dim cloud of the coming day and from where the sun promised to rise. Alabay turned from the faint shimmerings of the dawn to the other direction, where lay the dark ravine. He gazed further up to the mountains themselves – where the night was slowly filtering away onto the city from the height of the nearby mountains. Gathering the remainder of his strength, the dog set off down the hill to where he had been drawn all these years by his burdensome memories. He took the shortest route through kitchen gardens and courtyards, and soon his run had come to its destination. And there he was – the well-fed, impolite servant of the destroyer of their canine family – he with the rattling chain round his neck!

The dogs first growled like irreconcilable enemies. There was quite a lot of malice in the eyes of both of them. First to attack was chained Black Brow; he stepped back a little, threw back his well-fed muzzle, bared his teeth and dashed into the attack. But the insidious iron chain – guarantor of his well-being – pulled him back and prevented him from making sudden movements. He dashed hither and thither, howling and clawing at his kennel. The cold iron chain kept his movements within bounds.

Then the house dog tried a stratagem. He pretended to retreat and lay down by his kennel. Alabay took this as a sign of reconciliation and took several steps towards his brother. He lay down, too. But he almost paid for his trust. Black Brow rushed at him without any warning and seized his brother by the stump of his ear but was unable to hold on for long. Repulsing him with a powerful blow of his paws away from himself, Alabay, pouring blood, watched to see what his brother would do. He did not have to wait long. The other one made one more attempt aimed at dashing under his opponent and, seizing him from underneath by the throat, gnawing through his gullet. Evading this crafty attack, Alabay selected a safe distance and remained motionless. For some reason he was in no hurry to attack his enemy, and he stood and examined him attentively and painfully like the most precious creature. Perhaps that was why he was in no haste. But now, it seemed, he had made his final decision and made a move. His appearance was terrifying: he had transferred the weight of his whole body to his back paws, pressing them into the earth as if attempting to kick the ground away from him, straightening his powerful neck and thrusting his head forward. The pupils of his eyes were dilated, the muscles of his whole body were hardened as in his best years, and the salty taste of blood rushed into his teeth. Skewbald bared his teeth menacingly and his throat gurgled. Then it all happened in the twinkling of an eye. Alabay leapt up high and hung above his opponent, and in the same movement firmly seized him by the neck, closing his jaws so tight that he crunched his vertebrae. The chained dog responded to this with a heart-rending howl. He struggled in desperation to extricate himself from the embraces of inevitable death, but to no avail. The domesticated dog could not have known of this trick of Alabay's, devised through years of cruel street skirmishes. Even if he had known it, the collar would not have allowed him to repel such an impetuous attack. He tumbled backwards, Puny's obedient servant did not even realise what had happened to him – there was no time for that. Skewbald throttled him before he could come to his senses. A soft crunch, and it was all over. Black Brow twitched his paws and was at rest forever.

The dogs' bellowing had awakened the master of the house. The front door was opened and a little head poked out. A strange picture greeted him: Black Brow was lying there lifeless and some stray cur was sniffing his body. The master was enraged, and seizing a long stick, he rushed madly at the murderer. He hit the dog on the head with all his might. Alabay's ears buzzed. His eyes met the cowardly look of Puny, who owed him blood-money from long ago. The stray growled so loud that the master rushed like a jerboa of the steppes back into the house, slamming the door behind him. In safety he watched from the window the behaviour of the unknown dog, who was in no hurry to leave. He lowered his huge head over his lifeless victim and began to sniff him from head to paws, howling piteously as if weeping. Then he left the courtyard by way of the kitchen garden, slowly departing obliquely along the path leading to the ravine.

Puny rushed into the bedroom and gave his wife a careful account of the reason for the noise in the courtyard.

"Some rabid stray dog killed ours," he said, and then, looking at the ceiling, he grumbled:

"The way we fed and watered him and trained him to be a guard dog – and all for nothing!"

"Go back to sleep," his wife scolded, listening vaguely, sinking once more into her pre-morning doze. "He had become old and useless – we would have had to get rid of him somewhere."

Her husband stared at the ceiling.

"I should have kept another one of them," he continued vexedly, in a half-whisper to himself. "There was one, a pugnacious fellow, but he was not caught, I remember it clearly as if it were today, and then he disappeared. If I had caught him and trained him, it would have all been different."

***

Early in the morning, when the sun had risen into a cold sky, children from the neighbouring courtyards saw an enormous skewbald dog, lying lifeless on the very edge of the ravine, beyond the last house. The dog looked as if he were alive and just sleeping, but with open eyes. He had laid his shaggy head on his fore-paws and was staring at the city awakening far below. In the depth of his wise, big eyes, forever stilled, were reflected the homely nearby houses of the district – houses huddled together as if guilty towards somebody...

The Tale of Aypi

by Ak Welsapar

The Tale of Aypi follows the fate of a group of Turkmen fishermen dwelling on the coast of the Caspian Sea. The fear of losing their ancestral home looms over the entire village. This injustice is being made to look like a voluntary initiative on the part of the fishermen themselves, whilst the ruling powers cynically attempt to confiscate their land. One brave fisherman from the village rises up to confront them and fights for his native shore, as a response to an act of cruelty inflicted on a defenceless young woman centuries ago. This unjustly executed soul returns as a ghost during this troubled time to exact a terrible revenge on the men of the village.

The relationships among the characters mirror the eternal opposition between the forces of nature, with the intervention of mystical forces ratcheting up the tension.

Buy it > www.glagoslav.com

Maybe We're Leaving

by Jan Balaban

A young boy from the housing estates comes across a copse of old oaks to which he can escape, as to an oasis of calm. Although he may forget about it once he becomes an adult and "puts aside the things of childhood," it will remain a locus of balance, decades later, for a single mother struggling with the difficulties of raising the child she loves. A husband, on the lip of an ugly divorce, drives across town in the middle of the night to rescue his wife, abandoned by her lover, and then — as she falls asleep in the car — takes the long way home, to prolong a moment such as he has not experienced in years. An elderly doctor, self-diagnosed with Alzheimer's disease, makes use of the few precious moments of consciousness granted him each morning to pass on to his grandson what he has learned about life and living responsibly. Loss, and permanence, the ephemeral and the eternal, are common themes of Jan Balabán's collection of short stories Maybe We're Leaving, presented here in the English translation of Charles S. Kraszewski. With psychological insight that rivals the great novels of Fyodor Dostoevsky, the twenty-one linked narratives that make up the collection present us with everyday people, with everyday problems — and teach us to love and respect the former, and bear the latter.

Buy it > www.glagoslav.com

CONVERSATIONS BEFORE SILENCE:

THE SELECTED POETRY OF OLES ILCHENKO

An avid reader of English-language poets such as William Carlos Williams and Stanley Kunitz, Ilchenko is one of the best Ukrainian poets writing in free verse today. His poetry is associative, flitting, and fragmentary. At times he does not form complete sentences in his poems and links words together into phrases before shifting into another thought or idea. The language of his poetry has a tendency to collapse into itself, often forcing the reader to reevaluate a word or line, to reread a previous word to focus on the poet's inner logic. This fragmentary incompleteness and permeability mimics much the way human consciousness works without the filter of the written communicative convention of sentences and grammatical structure. This "slipperiness" and rapid shifting of voice comprises one of the essential invariants in Ilchenko's poetics. The poet also flaunts many traditional poetic Ukrainian conventions. Like ee cummings he tends to avoid capital letters or punctuation such as exclamation points. One will find only commas and dashes for pauses, and an occasional period in his poems, which do not always end with the finality of that punctuation mark...

Buy it > www.glagoslav.com

Forefathers' Eve

by Adam Mickiewicz

Forefathers' Eve [*Dziady*] is a four-part dramatic work begun circa 1820 and completed in 1832 – with Part I published only after the poet's death, in 1860. The drama's title refers to *Dziady*, an ancient Slavic and Lithuanian feast commemorating the dead. This is the grand work of Polish literature, and it is one that elevates Mickiewicz to a position among the "great Europeans" such as Dante and Goethe.

With its Christian background of the Communion of the Saints, revenant spirits, and the interpenetration of the worlds of time and eternity, *Forefathers' Eve* speaks to men and women of all times and places. While it is a truly Polish work – Polish actors covet the role of Gustaw/Konrad in the same way that Anglophone actors covet that of Hamlet – it is one of the most universal works of literature written during the nineteenth century. It has been compared to Goethe's Faust – and rightfully so...

Buy it > www.glagoslav.com

Acropolis – The Wawel Plays
by Stanisław Wyspiański

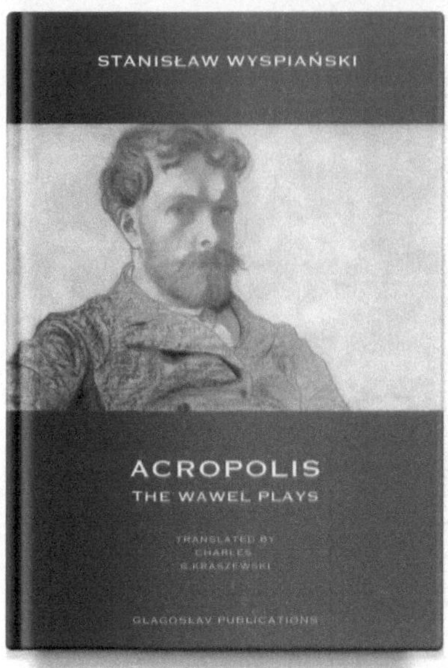

Stanisław Wyspiański (1869-1907) achieved worldwide fame, both as a painter, and Poland's greatest dramatist of the first half of the twentieth century. *Acropolis: the Wawel Plays*, brings together four of Wyspiański's most important dramatic works in a new English translation by Charles S. Kraszewski. All of the plays centre on Wawel Hill: the legendary seat of royal and ecclesiastical power in the poet's native city, the ancient capital of Poland. In these plays, Wyspiański explores the foundational myths of his nation: that of the self-sacrificial Wanda, and the struggle between King Bolesław the Bold and Bishop Stanisław Szczepanowski. In the eponymous play which brings the cycle to an end, Wyspiański carefully considers the value of myth to a nation without political autonomy, soaring in thought into an apocalyptic vision of the future. Richly illustrated with the poet's artwork, *Acropolis: the Wawel Plays* also contains Wyspiański's architectural proposal for the renovation of Wawel Hill, and a detailed critical introduction by the translator. In its plaited presentation of *Bolesław the Bold* and *Skałka*, the translation offers, for the first time, the two plays in the unified, composite format that the poet intended, but was prevented from carrying out by his untimely death.

Buy it > www.glagoslav.com

- *Solar Plexus* by Rustam Ibragimbekov
- *Don't Call me a Victim!* by Dina Yafasova
- *Poetin (Dutch Edition)* by Chris Hutchins and Alexander Korobko
- *A History of Belarus* by Lubov Bazan
- *Children's Fashion of the Russian Empire* by Alexander Vasiliev
- *Empire of Corruption - The Russian National Pastime* by Vladimir Soloviev
- *Heroes of the 90s - People and Money. The Modern History of Russian Capitalism*
- *Fifty Highlights from the Russian Literature (Dutch Edition)* by Maarten Tengbergen
- *Bajesvolk (Dutch Edition)* by Mikhail Khodorkovsky
- *Tsarina Alexandra's Diary (Dutch Edition)*
- *Myths about Russia* by Vladimir Medinskiy
- *Boris Yeltsin - The Decade that Shook the World* by Boris Minaev
- *A Man Of Change - A study of the political life of Boris Yeltsin*
- *Sberbank - The Rebirth of Russia's Financial Giant* by Evgeny Karasyuk
- *To Get Ukraine* by Oleksandr Shyshko
- *Asystole* by Oleg Pavlov
- *Gnedich* by Maria Rybakova
- *Marina Tsvetaeva - The Essential Poetry*
- *Multiple Personalities* by Tatyana Shcherbina
- *The Investigator* by Margarita Khemlin
- *The Exile* by Zinaida Tulub
- *Leo Tolstoy – Flight from paradise* by Pavel Basinsky
- *Moscow in the 1930* by Natalia Gromova
- *Laurus (Dutch edition)* by Evgenij Vodolazkin
- *Prisoner* by Anna Nemzer
- *The Crime of Chernobyl - The Nuclear Goulag* by Wladimir Tchertkoff
- *Alpine Ballad* by Vasil Bykau
- *The Complete Correspondence of Hryhory Skovoroda*

- *The Tale of Aypi* by Ak Welsapar
- *Selected Poems* by Lydia Grigorieva
- *The Fantastic Worlds of Yuri Vynnychuk*
- *The Garden of Divine Songs and Collected Poetry of Hryhory Skovoroda*
- *Adventures in the Slavic Kitchen: A Book of Essays with Recipes*
- *Seven Signs of the Lion* by Michael M. Naydan
- *Forefathers' Eve* by Adam Mickiewicz
- *One-Two* by Igor Eliseev
- *Girls, be Good* by Bojan Babić
- *Time of the Octopus* by Anatoly Kucherena
- *Soghomon Tehlirian Memories - The Assassination of Talaat*
- *The Grand Harmony* by Bohdan Ihor Antonych
- *The Selected Lyric Poetry Of Maksym Rylsky*
- *The Shining Light* by Galymkair Mutanov
- *The Frontier: 28 Contemporary Ukrainian Poets - An Anthology*
- *Acropolis - The Wawel Plays* by Stanisław Wyspiański
- *Contours of the City* by Attyla Mohylny
- *Conversations Before Silence: The Selected Poetry of Oles Ilchenko*
- *Nikolai Gumilev's Africa* by Nikolai Gumilev
- *Zinnober's Poppets* by Elena Chizhova
- *The Hemingway Game* by Evgeni Grishkovets
- *The Secret History of my Sojourn in Russia* by Jaroslav HašekCharles S. Kraszewski
- *Mirror Sand - An Anthology of Russian Short Poems in English Translation* (A Bilingual Edition)
- *Maybe We're Leaving* by Jan Balaban
- *A Brown Man in Russia - Perambulations Through A Siberian Winter* by Vijay Menon

More coming soon...

www.ingramcontent.com/pod-product-compliance
Lightning Source LLC
Chambersburg PA
CBHW032034180726
48284CB00008B/2587